RETRIBUTION

A Whitney Steel Novel - Book Two

Kim Cresswell

KC Publishing

Copyright © 2015 Kim Cresswell

Retribution/Kim Cresswell - 1st Edition
ISBN: 978-0-9920841-8-9

Cover design by KC Book Cover Design

Subscribe to Kim's quarterly newsletter so you don't miss out on exclusive content, deals, upcoming releases, first-to-see book covers, contests, freebies, and more at www.kimcresswell.ca.

For Justin, Carla, Porter, and Peyton
In memory of Mary Beech
Death leaves a heartache no one can heal, love leaves a
memory no one can steal. — From a headstone in Ireland

ABOUT THE AUTHOR

Kim Cresswell resides in Ontario, Canada and is the award-winning author of the action-packed WHITNEY STEEL series.

Her debut romantic thriller, *Reflection* (A Whitney Steel Novel - Book One) has won numerous awards: RomCon®'s 2014 Readers' Crown Finalist (Romantic Suspense), InD'tale Magazine 2014 Rone Award Finalist (Suspense/Thriller), UP Authors Fiction Challenge Winner, Silicon Valley's Romance Writers of America (RWA) "Gotcha!" Romantic Suspense Winner, and an Honorable Mention in Calgary's (RWA) The Writer's Voice Contest.

Kim signed a 3-book German translation deal with Luzifer Verlag for the first three books in the Whitney Steel series: *Reflection, Retribution,* and *Resurrect.* The popular series will be published in German beginning in 2018.

The Assassin Chronicles TV series, based on Kim's upcoming 4-book paranormal thriller series: *Deadly Shadow, Invisible Truth, Assassin's Prophecy,* and *Vision of Fire* was in development with Council Tree Productions.

Web Site: www.kimcresswell.ca

Facebook: www.facebook.com/KimCresswellBooks

Twitter: http://twitter.com/kimcresswell

ALSO BY KIM CRESSWELL

The Whitney Steel Series
Reflection (Book One)
Retribution (Book Two)
Resurrect (Book Three)

The Assassin Chronicles Series
Deadly Shadow (Book One)

The Sum of all Tears Series
Icehaven (Book One)
Liberty (Book Two)

The Raina Storm Thriller Series
Dawn of the Storm (Book One)
Dawn of the Enemy (Book Two)

Single Title Novellas
Lethal Journey

The True Crime Quickie Short Story Series
Real Life Evil
Murder on Sunset Strip

Garden of Bones
Edge of Madness
Chameleon
Backwoods Murder

Anthologies Published by Grinning Man Press
Serial Killer Quarterly "21st Century Psychos"
Serial Killer Quarterly "Partners in Pain"
Serial Killer Quarterly "Unsolved in North America"
Serial Killer Quarterly "Cruel Britannia"
Serial Killer Quarterly "They Almost Got Away"
Serial Killer Quarterly "Lostmord: Murder in German"

PRAISE FOR RETRIBUTION

"Retribution pulls the reader in from the first page and delivers twists until the very last word. The heartfelt romance between feisty protagonist Whitney Steel and FBI Agent Blake Barnett will leave romantic suspense readers desperate for more!" — Stacy Green, international bestselling author of *Tin God*

"Retribution is a wild and terrifying ride!" — Patricia, Room with Books

"Another fast-paced adventure filled with heart-pumping action, irresistible characters, and riveting scenes." — Kat Flannery, award winning author of *BLOOD CURSE*

"Using bold strokes and realistic scenarios, Ms. Cresswell takes us along on a chilling ride, being held by the minions of evil and in fear for our safety." — Dii, Tome Tender Book Blog

CHAPTER ONE

*D*eath by lethal injection.

Whitney had waited years to hear those four words. Final justice for a man who'd taken so much from her and her fiancé, Blake Barnett. She stood on the concrete steps outside the seven storey L-shaped courthouse waiting for her cameraman, Jerry Maxwell, to give her the on-air countdown. After a last-minute microphone check, Whitney drew a deep breath then exhaled slowly.

Jerry held up his fingers. "In five…four…three…two…one."

"I'm reporting live outside the district courthouse on South Las Vegas Boulevard. Moments ago, District Attorney Jason Kurz announced the jury had sentenced Nathan Shaw to death by lethal injection. Mr. Kurz stated the jury found, unanimously and beyond a reasonable doubt, that Mr. Shaw is a continuing threat to society."

She swallowed hard, barely able to get the words out.

"A month ago, Nathan Shaw, owner of ShawBioGen, was found guilty on four counts of conspiracy to commit murder and one count of attempted murder of a federal agent."

That FBI agent is the man I love.

The memory of that day was before her in all its

bloody horror. The image of Blake shot and left to die played over and over in her mind. Perspiration broke out across her forehead.

Damn it. Not now. Breathe...

"Mr. Shaw had hired a hitman to kill Claire Barnett, a microbiologist with his company, Senator Mason Bailey, George Raines, an editor with WBNN-TV, and District Attorney Kate Leathham in hopes of covering up his illegal human cloning project." Sadness tugged at her heart. So many lives lost. Her legs trembled. "Nathan Shaw will be executed at Nevada State Prison in Carson City. His attorney, Warren Demotteo, is expected to file a formal appeal later today."

She paused to take a breath. "This is Whitney Steel. News3."

Jerry gave a quick nod, his cue they were off the air.

Whitney lowered the microphone and kept it clutched in her right hand as she watched two workers at the other end of the courthouse dismantling the makeshift press conference tent used earlier.

"Are you okay?" Jerry removed the camera from his shoulder and placed it on the ground. "For a minute there, I thought you were going to pass out."

Her body went limp with relief. Her gaze met his. She smiled and picked up her purse from the step and swung it over her shoulder. "I'll be fine."

It's finally over.

With Nathan Shaw's sentencing behind her, now she could focus on her upcoming wedding on August second which was less than three weeks away. She couldn't wait. And neither could Blake.

In the parking lot, Jerry opened the rear door of the News3 satellite broadcast van and loaded their equipment.

Whitney eyed a white SUV with dark tinted windows stop a car's length away. With the lot full due to the sentencing, the driver appeared to be waiting for their spot.

Jerry slammed the van door shut. "You ready?"

"Yeah, let's get back to the station." She glanced over her shoulder.

Three men jumped out of the SUV wearing black balaclavas.

They barreled toward her.

She spotted guns in their hands.

After a brief moment of paralyzing disbelief, Whitney clutched her purse and bolted to the passenger side of the vehicle.

"Get in. Hurry!" Jerry yelled.

She reached for the door handle, but a strong arm looped around her neck and dragged her back.

The heels of her shoes scrapped against the pavement. "Let go—of me."

The man covered her mouth with a leather-gloved hand and pulled her between the parked cars and out of sight.

She felt the muzzle of the gun jab into her back.

Moist breath brushed against her ear. "Shut the hell up."

Another man held a gun to Jerry's temple. "You're going to film this. Live. Understand?"

Jerry held up his hands, his eyes wide. "Okay, okay. But—it's going to take a few minutes to setup the feed." He opened the van's back door again and fumbled for his equipment.

Whitney squirmed.

The man tightened his grip around her neck.

She wheezed and fought for a breath.

Who were these men? What did they want?

The sane voice in her head ordered her to stay still. Even though she had a black belt in karate and was skilled at crushing a person's windpipe or disarming a knife-wielding attacker, she wasn't stupid enough to take on three guys that were double her height and weight with guns aimed at her. All she could do was watch, stay as calm as possible, and hope someone would see what was going on and call the police.

When Jerry had the live feed setup, he stood in front of them, camera ready. His voice trembled. "You're on."

The third man, the tallest of the group, pulled a red and white bandana out of a small plastic bag he had stuffed in the pocket of his jeans.

He pressed the moist cloth over her mouth and nose and held it there.

She squirmed and kicked but it was useless. Her head started to buzz. The sickly, sweet smell mixed with the rotten odor of strong cleaning solution invaded her head.

Blood pounded in her ears and male voices turned faint and distorted.

As her breathing slowed every muscle turned to mush. Then blackness drowned her vision and she realized what the men wanted.

They wanted her.

CHAPTER TWO

In SecuraCorp's conference room, Blake pushed aside his empty coffee mug on the table and cracked his knuckles. His business partner, Mike Jacobs, sat in silence across from him.

Monday morning's good news about Nathan Shaw's death sentence had been abruptly overshadowed by a handwritten letter demanding a million dollars.

Vic Serrano, a computer forensics examiner with the FBI's Cyber Action Team, walked in with a grim expression on his face.

He tossed a file folder on the table then rolled the sleeves of his white dress shirt to his elbows before he sat. "It's confirmed. Someone hacked into the network at two thirty-two this morning."

Blake slammed his hand down on the table. "Christ."

Their confidential client files had been compromised and the blackmailer was threatening to print the personal details in every major newspaper—a move which could destroy their business.

"Crossman and Hamlin are analyzing the code, looking for IP addresses, email addresses, clues that could lead us to the person or persons responsible. It's going to take a bit of time."

Time they didn't have.

Even though Blake and Mike had officially left the FBI immediately after the Nathan Shaw case and started an investigation-security firm, off the record, both agents were still on the books and called upon by the Bureau for delicate covert operations. And some of those files were on the company's main computer.

He stared at the blackmail letter in a clear plastic evidence bag.

This wasn't a joke. It was real. The outcome would not only destroy their business but would put a handful of undercover FBI agents at risk—agents with families. Agents he and Mike had worked with for years.

Blake's stomach churned. His chest ached where Nathan Shaw had shot him three years ago. A pain he'd thought was long gone.

Mike leaned forward in his chair. "What are we going to do? We've got less than twenty-four hours."

Vic piped up. "My advice. Hang tight. Let Crossman and Hamlin work their magic. Tim Hamlin might look like a high school kid but he's a genius. The best in our unit." He stood, and then walked to the door. "I'll let you know what the guys find."

"Thanks." Blake watched the man exit the room and close the door behind him. "Why today? The same day Nathan Shaw was sentenced?"

"Are you thinking what I'm thinking—that this blackmail scheme somehow involves Nathan Shaw?" Mike asked.

A headache pounded behind Blake's eyes. He rubbed his forehead hoping to relieve some of the pain. "It sure as hell wouldn't surprise me. Not as if the guy has anything to lose."

If there was one thing Blake had learned during the

past few years, there was no such thing as a coincidence when Nathan Shaw's name cropped up. None.

The bastard was responsible for over a half-dozen deaths including Blake's sister, Claire, Whitney's ex-husband, Mason, and her good friend, George. All dead because Nathan wanted to keep his human cloning project hidden from the world. The man had even gone so far as conspiring with a ghost from Blake's past, Pablo Sanchez, once a top leader with the Sur del Calle cartel, Colombia's largest drug trafficking organization.

Together Shaw and Sanchez had concocted a plan to kidnap Angel, the world's first cloned human, the same sweet young girl Blake and Whitney were waiting to adopt. Luckily, the kidnap plan backfired and afterwards, Sanchez had escaped the US.

According to sources, he was hiding in Bogotá, shielded by guerrillas and the money-lined pockets of the National Police. There was no chance in hell he'd be returned to the United States to stand trial on kidnapping charges, nor for the death of Kate Leatham, Las Vegas' previous district attorney.

The door flew open.

Blake's secretary blew into the room. "Oh, my God. You need to see this. It's all over the news."

He didn't have a chance of stopping the cyclone-of-a-woman from interrupting, something she did on a regular basis. His muscles tensed. He glanced at Mike.

His partner shrugged as if to say, 'Hey, you hired her pal.'

God damn it. Enough was enough. Blake stood. "Michelle. Not now."

Ignoring him, she raced to the far end of the room, grabbed the remote from the shelf, and turned on the flat screen television.

"You have to see this." She pointed to the screen. "It's Whitney."

Mike bounced up knocking his chair to the floor.

Blake froze.

Navy pants and jacket...white v-neck top.

He shook his head in disbelief.

Brown hair covered her forehead; her green eyes were wide with terror. The tall man holding her on the right put a red rag over her mouth. She struggled and kicked. A few moments later, her head bobbed forward then back again before her body went limp.

Blake clenched his fists so tight, his knuckles turned white.

Another man stood to the left. He raised a gun and pointed at the camera. "Shut it off, now."

The screen went black.

The audio was still on.

A single gunshot.

A man cried out in pain.

Michelle's hand flew over her mouth. She gasped. "Oh, my God."

Blake recognized the man's pinched voice. Jerry Maxwell, Whitney's cameraman.

Another male voice said, "Get out of here!"

An engine snarled.

Seconds later, tires screeched.

A short, silent pause.

A female reporter came into view. "The woman is identified as Whitney Steel, a reporter here at News3." Her voice quivered slightly. "Miss Steel and Blake Barnett, a former FBI Special Agent, were instrumental in putting Nathan Shaw behind bars. Earlier this morning,

Mr. Shaw received the death sentence. Jerry Maxwell, who shot the footage, was rushed to University Medical Center where he's undergoing emergency surgery for a gunshot wound to his right thigh."

The reporter paused to brush the hair out of her face. "At the moment, authorities are tight-lipped, only saying their investigation is ongoing."

Blake felt Mike's hand on his shoulder. "She'll be okay. We'll find her."

"Damn right we will." Blake heard the tremble in his voice. He forced himself to focus. Whitney's life depended on him keeping it together. "Michelle, get Trent Chambers on the phone. Mike, round up McBride and Cally. Have McBride come here in case the blackmailer calls. Oh, and let Vic know what's going on."

His secretary nodded.

"You got it," Mike said.

With the room empty, Blake drew a deep breath and sat down. His hands shook.

The wedding. The adoption.

I'll find you, baby. I promise.

He stared at the blackmail letter. A half hour ago that damn piece paper was urgent. Not anymore.

Only one thing mattered—finding Whitney.

❈ ❈ ❈

Forty minutes east of Las Vegas, behind the abandoned Chevron gas station, Cortez Guerrero watched Raul and Enzo load the unconscious woman into the green van.

They were ditching the white SUV, and then backtracking west. Their destination, a cargo ship in San Diego heading to Tumaco, Colombia. From there, they'd travel by rail to Bogotá.

He punched the number into the throw-away cell phone and waited for Pablo to answer.

On the third ring, the man picked up. "Yes."

"We have the woman."

"Good work, Hermano."

Cortez grinned. It always amused him when Pablo called him, brother. They were like brothers, both abandoned by their parents at the age of twelve, left to survive in the sewers beneath the streets of Bogotá.

Don't think about those days.

But he couldn't forget about the revolting stench of urine, feces, and death or sleeping with a knife clutched in his hand especially when the death squads came down the pipes to shoot at them or rape...

Stop thinking. Things are different now.

"Everything went as planned. We'll be at the port tonight."

"Have a safe trip, my brother. I will see you by the end of the week."

The call ended.

To Cortez, this was just a job like one of many in the past and one which paid much more than most. Five hundred thousand US dollars.

He dropped the cell phone at his feet in the gravel and stomped it with the heel of his boot until it broke into pieces. After lighting a cigarette, he took a long drag and thought about his twenty-three-year-old brother, Alberto, locked up in prison. The man would be almost forty by the time he was released. A sad reality.

It was odd standing here, the exact spot where his brother had been shot in the stomach. Cortez felt bad he'd only visited Alberto once, but he couldn't afford to draw attention to himself. Not now. Not when Pablo had spent months putting his plan in place.

Cortez pushed the thought away and waved signaling they were ready to go. What was Pablo planning on doing with the woman?

Not sure if he really wanted to know the answer, he flicked what was left of his cigarette and hurried to the van.

❋ ❋ ❋

Whitney swallowed hard, her throat scratchy and dry. She pried her eyes open.

How long had she been unconscious? Days? Hours?

Daylight forced her to squint as nausea mixed with vertigo. She snapped her lids shut and inhaled then exhaled slowly until her head stopped spinning and the nausea dissipated. The last thing she remembered was being in the courthouse parking lot with Jerry...the men...chloroform.

She opened her eyes.

Now she was sitting with her hands cuffed in her lap. Her ankles were bound together with a thick wad of duct tape. At some point the three men had removed their ski masks, revealing olive skin and brown hair clipped short, military style. Panic surged through her. *Oh, God. They weren't concerned she could identify them.*

"She's awake," the man in the passenger seat said.

The driver peered over his shoulder then to the road ahead.

A few seconds later the driver glanced back again. "Raul, give her some water."

His stony blue eyes made her shiver. They also didn't care if she knew their names. She wiggled and struggled against the seat belt.

The man sitting in the seat in front of her, apparently Raul, turned. A thin almost unnoticeable scar ran from above his right eye to the corner of his mouth. He passed an open bottle of water over the seat.

Whitney tried to lift her hands, but they refused to budge. A side effect of the chloroform?

Come on. She tried again. This time, she was able to grasp the bottle.

After managing to take a few sips, her dry mouth and throat sucked up the fluid and demanded more. She downed the rest of the water.

Panic took over, again. Her hands trembled in her lap.

Where were they?

She stared out the tinted window. Vehicles zoomed by. According to the signs they were on Highway 160, heading west, which meant she'd been unconscious for less than an hour.

Minutes later, they turned on to Interstate 95, heading north along the Nevada Test Site where hundreds of nuclear tests had taken place in the fifties until the early nineties.

Whitney knew the area well. Too well.

Adjacent to the site was Nellis Air Force Base. A shiver rocketed through her body. She thought of Blake and how Nathan Shaw had almost taken him away from her.

Whitney moved from the window and paced the empty office located in Area 1 of Nellis Air Force Base. Down the hall and to the right, the rest of Blake's FBI team had gathered in private.

Her stomach winced. The waiting was killing her.

She checked her watch for the fiftieth time. Where was Blake? He should have been here by now. Two hours had passed since she'd left him at the facility, bleeding.

I didn't have a choice. I had to leave you, to save Angel.

She rushed to Mike the moment he walked through the door. Immediately, she noticed the somber expression on his face.

Her body trembled. "Any word?"

Mike shook his head. "Nothing yet. We should know something soon."

She had to ask even though the thought was unbearable. "You don't think he's dead, do you?"

"No. He's too damn tough."

That may be, but Whitney had seen how much blood he'd lost. More than she thought possible. Anything could have happened after she had fled with Angel. That poor child would have nightmares after what she'd witnessed. Right now, the little girl was being looked after at the hospital on base.

Whitney flinched, startled by the ring of Mike's cell phone. She held her breath as he answered the call.

Please be good news.

Mike's expression changed…but she couldn't read him.

"Yeah, thanks." He shut off his phone. "They just brought Blake in. He's unconscious, lost a lot of blood. Things don't look good, Whitney."

The twang of country music coming from the van's radio dragged her back to the present.

She'd been abducted and didn't know by whom or why.

"How much longer before we're in California?" the man in the passenger seat asked the driver.

California? Fear spiraled up and her heart pounded triple time. She couldn't allow them to take her out of the state. She had to do something and quick.

"Soon, Enzo. Soon," the driver said as he turned the

radio down.

On the seat beside her, Whitney eyed her shoulder bag. Her cell phone. She had turned off the ringer before going on air. Had the men found it? Whitney prayed they hadn't. She needed to get a message to Blake and let him know where she was. It might be her only chance.

Looking straight ahead, she carefully inched the bag closer and slipped her hands inside.

"Is this what you're looking for?" The driver held up her cell phone. He opened the window and tossed out the phone.

Her heart stopped. *No!*

Raul turned and stared at her.

The breath sucked out of her lungs when she noticed what was etched on the driver's right hand at the base of his thumb.

A small serpent tattoo. The same tattoo Pablo Sanchez had on his neck.

It wouldn't be long before she was dead.

CHAPTER THREE

E ach time Blake witnessed the fear in Whitney's eyes in his mind, another piece of his heart shattered. He slammed his palm against the steering wheel. "God damn it. I have to find her."

This wasn't a random act. It was personal—a message to him. If it wasn't, then why film it? Why waste the extra time and risk getting caught?

Before he'd left the office, the conference room had been transformed into a makeshift command center. Was Whitney's abduction related to the blackmail letter he'd received? Blake couldn't help but wonder. He was supposed to be by her side when the judge handed down Nathan Shaw's sentencing. Instead, he stayed at the office to deal with the blackmail issue.

A diversion? Had the abductors wanted to keep him out of the way to make it easier to snatch Whitney? The timing was perfect.

Too perfect.

Blake hoped the crime scene would give him some answers. He drew a deep, unsteady breath, grabbed his cell phone from the passenger seat of the pickup truck, and opened the door.

News crews prowled the sidewalk in front of the courthouse and went on high alert the second he hopped out of the truck. He ran across Las Vegas Boulevard.

"Is the FBI officially involved in your fiancée's disappearance?" asked a reporter.

He clutched the cell phone tighter. It wasn't a disappearance. She was bloody-well taken.

The same reporter tried again. "Do the authorities have any leads?"

Blake ignored the questions and kept walking at a brisk pace. At the police barricade, he showed his ID, and a female officer logged him into the scene. He shoved one hand into his jeans pocket and kept a death grip on his phone with the other in case Whitney or the kidnappers called.

Inside the cordoned off area, cars lined both sides of the lot at least twelve rows deep. Someone had to have seen something.

A handful of crime scene analysts were busy collecting and documenting evidence while others were photographing and videotaping the scene. A few feet away, next to the white and blue News3 truck, Trent Chambers silver hair and thin face stood out in the flurry of activity. Blake went to meet him.

"I just finished with Detective Willis. The locals aren't too happy we're taking over," Trent said.

"They never are when the Bureau is involved." Blake stared at the truck and tried to imagine how terrified Whitney must have been—must still be.

He wiped the sweat from his forehead with the back of his hand. "Have we got anything useful?"

"Cigarette butts, pop cans, a couple parking receipts, a 9mm shell casing, and lots of prints inside and outside of the news van. Probably Whitney's and Maxwell's. The good news is one of the courthouse security cameras outside might have picked up something. Mike's checking it right now."

"Good. Did anyone see what the men were driving?" Blake wasn't as calm as he sounded. His heart threatened to explode from his chest.

"The locals are interviewing possible witnesses. With all the activity here this morning with the Shaw case someone had to have seen something."

He hoped Chambers was right.

Blake's phone rang. Both men froze. He looked at the caller ID.

"It's just Mike." Blake wasn't sure if he was relieved or disappointed. He answered the call.

"We just got lucky, man. We're looking for a 2000 white GMC Jimmy. The vehicle entered the lot at nine thirty-seven. The men drove around for about four minutes, stopped a couple car lengths away from where Whitney and Jerry were parked. The men appear to be all the same height and weight. Looks like one of them might have tossed something. Maybe a cigarette butt. Security's making a copy of the tape right now. Hang in there. We're going to find her."

"Yup, we are." They had to. "When you're done, meet me across the street from the courthouse. I want to the go hospital and talk to Jerry."

"Will do," Mike said.

Blake ended the call. For the first time, he had real hope. At least now they had something to go on; a vehicle, and possibly the DNA of one of the abductors. But he couldn't shake the worry in his gut. He turned to Chambers who had just finished talking to one of the local cops. Even though the man had been his SAC for almost fifteen years, Chambers had agreed to let Blake run the show. Besides, Chambers had learned the hard way when Angel had been kidnapped by Pablo Sanchez three years before that Blake would do whatever was necessary. He'd also do whatever was necessary to find Whitney. No one could or would stop him, and Chambers knew it.

"We're looking for a white GMC Jimmy." Blake stared at the bloodstained patch of pavement drying in the sun where Jerry had been shot.

"I'll have Willis issue an APB."

"We need a rush on the evidence too. Have the lab check the cigarette butts first for DNA. Mike thinks one of the men was smoking. Let me know what CODIS comes up with."

"Okay." Blake felt Chambers hand on his shoulder. "If you need anything else, let me know."

Blake was taken aback. He had never seen this side of the man. "I will. Thanks." He turned and started back toward the police barricade when his phone rang again.

He stopped and looked at the number. It wasn't familiar.

The abductors? Whitney?

On the third ring, he pressed the talk button. "Hello."

"We have a collect call from Nathan Shaw. Will you accept the charges?" a female voice asked.

Blake's mouth dropped open. Now the bastard was contacting him from prison. "You *have got* to be kidding."

"Sir, will you accept the charges?" the woman asked again.

He gritted his teeth. "Yes."

A few seconds of silence passed before the operator said, "Go ahead, Mr. Shaw."

"Too bad about our lovely Miss Steel."

✳ ✳ ✳

Whitney's mind reeled, the image of the tattoo fresh in her mind. Her body shook from the inside out, causing the metal handcuffs to clink together. She caught the driver glancing at her from the rear-view mirror. She looked away and stared down at her diamond engagement ring and remembered what Blake had said three years ago, the same day he had proposed.

"Don't worry. Sanchez is on every US watch list. We're safe. He wouldn't risk coming back here."

Wrong. She was far from safe. Pablo Sanchez was back to finish what he'd started.

She needed to find a way to escape.

Whitney watched Enzo shift in the passenger seat and lean his head back on the headrest.

Even if she could get the van door open they were traveling at least seventy miles an hour. She'd die for sure.

Raul held up another open bottle of water for her.

She hesitated for a moment, then grabbed the bottle and drank all of it. She peered out the window. Her heart sank.

They were already in California.

In the middle of nowhere. The Mojave Desert.

About five miles southwest of Baker, the van slowed. Palm trees towered forty feet high looking like guards ushering her to her death.

Whitney spotted the green and white Zzyzx Road sign.

Her mind drifted back to when she was eleven, a year after her mother had been killed by a drunk driver when Whitney and her father had taken one of their special weekend road trips. Something they did together whenever he wasn't out of the country on assignment.

Whitney pointed over the dashboard. "Look, daddy. Z-z-y-z-x. What a funny name for a road."

Her father grinned. "Honey, it's pronounced, Zeye-zix. It rhymes with "Isaac's."

She giggled. "It's still a funny name."

The van heaved to the left and jolted Whitney.

Her father had been killed on assignment in Colombia in nineteen ninety-seven and to this day, she never knew what he had been working on. No one did. Was his death connected to Pablo Sanchez and the Sur del Calle cartel? She shivered at the thought.

Suddenly paved road dropped out beneath the vehicle.

Each time the van hit a bump on the dirt road the seatbelt tightened across her shoulder and chest. In the distance, across the dry lakebed, she eyed the Zzyzx peninsula. Miles of barren desert and rock. Welcome to hell.

I have to find a way out of this. Think. Whitney stared at the back of Raul's head.

Then it hit her.

She twisted her hands in her lap and checked her watch. If the men were heading to Barstow, they were maybe less than an hour away. At least they'd be in a city. Slower traffic. People. A chance to get someone's attention or escape.

She knew what she had to do.

CHAPTER FOUR

Nathan Shaw had a lot of nerve. Would the bastard ever be out of their lives? Not until he was dead. And that couldn't come soon enough.

Blake gritted his teeth. "What the hell do you want?"

"To offer my condolences, of course. Poor Miss Steel. She looked absolutely terrified on TV."

"You'd better hope you aren't involved because if anything happens to her..." Blake forced himself to stop. The last thing he should do was threaten Shaw especially when the conversation was being monitored and recorded by prison officials.

I don't have time for this crap. Fear reached deep in his gut and rose in his throat. "Don't call me again."

"I have some information which may interest you. It's about Miss Steel."

Typical Nathan. Cocky, arrogant, and manipulating any situation to his advantage. Not this time. Blake didn't believe a word the man said. "Bullshit."

Before ending the call, he heard Nathan say, "You know where I am."

Yeah. In a holding cell waiting to be transferred back to prison, you murdering bastard.

Blake kicked gravel beneath his feet, his mind ready to explode. What if Shaw really knew something that could help find Whitney? What if he didn't and valuable time was wasted?

He spotted Mike darting across Las Vegas Boulevard from the courthouse. At six-four, Mike was stocky and intimidating. Not someone you would want to run into in a dark alley. He looked like a hulking bounty hunter or an undercover cop.

Mike stopped and gasped for a breath. "Hey. Just got word the locals found an abandoned white SUV. They're positive it's the vehicle the abductors used. You won't believe where."

Finally, a lead. Blake looked at his partner. "Where?"

"Behind the same Chevron gas station where we had our last run-in with Pablo Sanchez."

He felt as if a bullet slammed into his chest. Blake scrubbed a hand over his face, not wanting to believe what he just heard.

Pablo Sanchez was back.

His biggest fear had come true.

If Whitney wasn't dead. She would be soon.

✲ ✲ ✲

How had Sanchez managed to get back into the US when he was on every watch list, including the FBI's most wanted? Blake couldn't shake the gut-wrenching terror building deep in his stomach—the unmistakable feeling of impending doom.

Nathan Shaw's words played over in his mind.

"I have some information that may interest you. About Miss Steel."

He didn't have a choice. He was forced to tolerate Shaw because he had to. Because if Blake didn't and something happened to Whitney...he would never forgive himself.

❊ ❊ ❊

"It's been an hour." Blake shook his head. "I don't like this one bit."

"Neither do I." Mike leaned against the wall and crossed his feet. "What do you think is taking so long?"

"I don't know." Blake cracked his knuckles and paced the length of the room. "But Shaw had better be on the up and up."

The door swung open.

Warren Demotteo, Nathan Shaw's attorney, walked in followed by Jason Kurtz, the district attorney.

Blake stopped pacing and turned to Kurtz. "What the hell is going on?"

"I have no idea." The DA set his briefcase on the scratched wood table then pulled out a chair. "Mr. Shaw requested we all be present."

Blake quickly digested the news. What the hell was Nathan up to? He glared at Kurtz. "When did you start giving in to that bastard?"

"The moment Whitney was abducted." Kurtz took a seat at the table. "At this point, we don't have a choice, do we? Besides, we don't have anything to lose by hearing what he has to say."

Shaw's attorney took a seat across from the DA, remained silent, and placed his briefcase on the floor next to his chair. Minutes later, a guard escorted Nathan into the room with his feet shackled and his hands cuffed in front of him.

The wide-eyed weirdo looked like shit. What hair was left on his balding head looked wiry and messy, his hundred-dollar haircuts long gone. Dark circles were prominent under his black-button beady eyes. The guy had the face of a stuffed squirrel. He appeared aged and worn. Good. At least Blake felt a wee bit of satisfaction knowing prison life was taking a toll.

Before the guard left the room, he pulled out a chair.

Nathan sat.

Blake wasn't waiting a second longer. "I'm tired of your games. Tell us what you know."

Nathan smirked. "It's not really that easy."

Warren Demotteo put his hand on Nathan's arm. "What my client is trying to say is he expects something in return for this information."

A deal? Anger bubbled in Blake's veins. His muscles tensed. He looked Shaw straight in the eyes. "What do you want?"

"A life sentence instead of the death penalty would be a good start."

Mike stepped away from the wall and burst out laughing. "After everything you've done, you have got to be joking. Do we have to remind you how many people you have killed?"

Shaw leaned back in the chair. "Take it or leave it. But just remember Miss Steel's life is at stake."

Blake stepped toward Nathan. Mike instinctively sidestepped in front of him. If he hadn't, Blake would have leapt across the table and beat the smirk off Shaw's face. He forced himself to calm down. "I know that, asshole. I also know your little cell mate Pablo Sanchez is involved."

The expression on Shaw's face didn't change. No look of surprise. Just a blank stare.

"But what's more important is I know exactly where he's taking Miss Steel." His bushy eyebrows rose and his mouth twisted. "Well, do we have a deal, gentlemen?"

The district attorney stood. "That's not going to happen." He straightened his suit jacket. "We're done here."

Blake felt as if he'd been hit in the knees with a baseball bat. He turned to the DA. "Let's talk in the hall."

"Yes, of course." Kurtz grabbed his briefcase from the table.

The hall was empty except for the guard standing outside the conference room.

"Do you have any clue how dangerous Sanchez is? Christ. He and his cartel have participated in the social cleansing of thousands of prostitutes, children, thieves, and the homeless just to name a few. And that was just for fun. Not to mention kidnapping Angel and murdering the previous district attorney." His hands balled into fists. "Jason, he'll kill Whitney. Can you live with that? I can't—I won't."

"Look, Blake. I'm fully aware of your past with Sanchez, but you know I can't give in to Nathan's demand. We've all worked too hard to ensure he received the death penalty. There's no turning back. At this point, we're not even sure Whitney is alive. I pray she is." He paused for a moment. "I really am sorry." The DA drew a deep breath and walked away.

Stunned, Blake peered through the small hallway window at the gray sky. Fear surged through him.

He wasn't going to lose the woman he loved. He couldn't.

He'd have to find another way.

❋ ❋ ❋

Moisture broke out on Whitney's forehead, despite the air conditioning blasting cool air throughout the van. She placed the empty water bottle at her feet and thought about Blake.

God, she loved him. He'd be worried sick. She also knew he wouldn't expect her to just sit back and be led to her demise without putting up one heck of a fight— a fight she planned on winning. There was no time for doubt.

I can do this. I have to.

The van slowed. Ahead, she spotted the welcome sign to Barstow. It might not be a huge city, population of twenty-five thousand at the most, but large enough to draw attention to the van—to her.

She moved her fingers under her thigh and grasped the five-inch nail file. Her heart raced. Staring at the back of Raul's thick neck one last time, her muscles tensed.

This was her chance.

She straightened, and then slowly leaned forward.

A little closer.

Her gaze darted to the rear-view mirror in case the driver was watching.

He wasn't.

The seatbelt clicked tight across her shoulder and chest and prevented her from going any further. She slid her high heels off.

I can do this.

Two captors were better than three. She'd take them out one by one if she had to.

Pablo Sanchez would not get the chance to kill her.

With both hands, she jabbed the nail file deep into the side of his neck and stabbed him repeatedly.

Blood squirted onto her hand and splattered down the back of the green seat.

Raul howled in pain. "Stop the crazy bitch!" His hands

flew to his neck trying to protect himself.

The driver looked over his shoulder. "Enzo, stop her!"

The van swerved into the other lane, and then back.

Whitney kept stabbing at his neck and hands.

The vehicle veered into the traffic again. Horns honked.

Raul gasped. "Help—me."

Enzo undid his seatbelt and lunged over the passenger seat.

He tried to grab her hand but missed.

With the last thrust, the file bent. Whitney dropped the piece of metal into her lap and threw her cuffed hands over the man's head. She yanked backwards with all her strength and braced her bound feet against the back of the seat for leverage. While the man thrashed and fought against her, strength drained from her body. For a brief moment, she wanted to give up. Instead, she closed her eyes and focused on Blake, their wedding and adopting Angel, the life that was waiting for her.

Finally, Raul stopped thrashing and his body went limp. His head slumped forward.

Whitney felt the adrenaline that had kept her going drain from her body. She opened her eyes and removed her hands from the man's neck. The barrel of a 9mm gun was aimed at her forehead.

Every muscle in her body turned to stone.

Cortez grasped Enzo's forearm. "Don't. Pablo wants her alive. His exact orders must be followed. Put the weapon away."

Whitney shrunk back into the seat, her hands sticky with blood and her wrists sore and bruised from the metal cuffs. The trauma of what she had just done kicked in. Her body shook uncontrollably.

"Look what the bitch did to him. We have to get him to a hospital. He's bleeding to death."

The driver was silent for a long moment. He looked at her, then back at Enzo.

"He's my brother, Cortez. I'm begging. We can't leave him here to die. We can drop him off in that town we just passed so he can get help. At least he'd have a chance."

"Enzo. You know better than anyone. Sometimes there are casualties in war. I'm sorry. This is one of those times."

Whitney looked away. She was determined not to be a casualty. At least she had one thing on her side. Pablo wanted her alive—which bought time to plan her next move.

CHAPTER FIVE

Blake sat in the swivel-chair and stared at his open laptop. He needed a few minutes to himself in his office to think, to clear his head. Nathan's words played over in his mind.

"I know where he's taking, Miss Steel."

Where the hell was Pablo taking her? Blake wished he knew. The nerve of Shaw to ask for a deal after everything he'd done and everyone he'd killed.

Blake thought about Claire and how much he missed having his sister in his life.

She was funny and geeky, a brilliant molecular biologist who'd worked for Nathan Shaw until he decided to have her killed because she had threatened to expose his human cloning project. At first, her death had been ruled accidental, but Blake refused to believe his sister would ever get on a boat since she was terrified of water and didn't know how to swim. And he was right. Under Nathan Shaw's orders, someone had lured her to the marina and blocked the exhaust outlets, allowing carbon monoxide to accumulate inside the cabin and poison her.

I can't lose Whitney too.

He snatched his cell phone from the desk and hit speed dial.

He'd been calling Whitney's phone non-stop. Each time he left a message telling her how much he loved her and that he would find her. But this time there was eerie silence on the other end. Nothing.

Bile crept up his throat.

The GPS was activated on her phone but determining where she was would take time. They could use trilateration to home in on her location between at least three satellites.

If she could just find a way to let him know she was okay.

Mike rushed into the room with a stack of papers in his hand. "The warden faxed over the visitor's logs for Shaw and Pablo's cousin."

He handed Blake the printouts. "Shaw's only visitor was his lawyer. Looks like Alberto had three."

Blake scanned the papers.

Mike pulled up a chair and sat. He pointed to the first name. "Adalene Lopez. She's the girlfriend."

Blake noted her visits stopped a month after Alberto had been incarcerated. "Looks like she's the ex-girlfriend now."

"Appears that way." Mike flipped to the next page. "His mother visited once a week. Every week. But look here." He pointed to a name on the list.

Blake's jaw tightened. "One visit, two weeks ago. Cortez Guerrero. Alberto's brother."

"I had the locals issue a BOLO for Guerrero and Sanchez. Cally's questioning the ex-girlfriend and the parents. Hopefully, we can catch a lead." Mike stood. "Chambers called too. He said he'd have your parents and Angel brought here before moving them to the safe house on Harmon."

Blake thought about the sweet little girl with blue eyes and a contagious giggle. The same girl he and Whitney had grown to love and were planning to adopt. To this day, no one other than a handful of FBI agents knew Angel was the world's first cloned human—an identical copy of Blake's sister Claire. She was six and a half years old and smart as hell. The less anyone knew about her, the better. The last thing they needed was a whirlwind of media hounds sniffing around and learning the truth.

His father was going to be angry considering this was the second time in three years they'd had their lives disrupted because of Pablo Sanchez.

Mike set his hand on Blake's shoulder. "You know every available agent is out there looking for her. We will find her."

Blake's gut wrenched. He didn't want to think about a life without her. "We have to, Mike."

After Mike left, Blake made a call to Hal Decker, an ex-marine buddy, former agent, and an expert in his own right.

The man picked up after the second ring. "Hello."

"Hey Hal, it's been awhile."

"Blake, sorry to hear about Whitney. What can I do?"

Clearly, the man had heard the news. "I need a search. 157 Howard Street. The house belongs to Sanchez's cousin."

Blake knew it wasn't a legal search. At this point, he didn't give a shit. He'd do anything to find Whitney.

"As in Pablo Sanchez?"

The thought made his chest ache. Blake drew a shaky breath. "Yes."

"Shit."

He knew exactly what Hal meant. She's a dead woman. Blake refused to give in to the idea. "I need bugs and surveillance. Whatever it takes." He leaned forward in the chair. "I've got to find something to work with, Hal."

"You got it, man. I'll load up and be at the house in forty-five."

"Thanks." Blake ended the call and set his phone on the desk.

Vic Serrano poked his head in the door. "Hate to bother you with everything else going on. The Whiz Kid cracked some code. It looks like the hacker used the Eye Tears virus to attack and decrypt the network password then copied three folders on the hard drive. He knew what he was looking for. We got a partial IP address. We're getting closer. It's slow going, though. I'll let you know when we have something concrete."

With Whitney missing, Blake had forgotten about the blackmailer. He eyed the clock on his laptop. In less than twenty hours he was expected to pay the ransom. "Keep me posted."

"I will." Vic paused for a long moment as if he wanted to say something but changed his mind before he disappeared down the hall.

The longer Blake thought about it the more he was convinced Whitney's abduction and the blackmail attempt were connected. If it hadn't been for someone hacking into the network, he would have been at the courthouse and he could have saved her.

Blake stood and stared out the window. *I should have been there.*

If anything happened to her, he would rip Pablo Sanchez apart with his bare hands.

When he turned, his secretary was standing in the doorway. "There's a call on line two. He said it's urgent and won't give me his name."

For God sakes, I don't need this right now. "Take a message."

"I tried—"

He held up his hand. "This isn't the time, Michelle." He knew his tone sounded harsh but right now his mind was on overload.

"The man said to tell you, 'Seventeen hours. Ticktock.'"

"Shit."

Blake ran past Michelle and down the hall to the conference room.

Paul McBride sat with his feet up on the corner of the two-drawer file cabinet, reading a computer magazine. At six-foot-three and built like a grizzly bear, the FBI agent usually looked much younger than forty-five years old. This morning he appeared older with a day's growth of hair on his cheeks and chin, his short blond hair uncombed. The stress of Whitney's abduction and the blackmail attempt was taking a toll on everyone.

"We're on," Blake said.

McBride hopped to his feet. After a few seconds, he nodded and gave Blake the thumbs-up to answer the call.

Blake stood beside him, snapped up the receiver, and hit the flashing 'line two' button. "Barnett."

"Do you have the money yet?"

It was clear from the metallic and digitized sound that the caller was using some type of electronic voice changer to disguise his voice which meant the person on the other end could possibly be a woman or even a kid. Christ, it could be anyone.

Blake just needed the caller to stay on the line long enough to trace the call. "I'm working on it. Takes time to raise a million dollars cash. How the hell do I know you're for real and not some lunatic playing games?"

There was a long pause of silence as if the phone had cut-out before the caller said, "Crackerbox."

Shit. The caller knew the Bureau's codename for the recent covert political corruption sting to nail a Vegas state senator with mob ties, a case Blake, Mike, and two other FBI agents had worked on for more than three months. Some of the details of the mission were on the main computer, including the real names of the other agents involved. Jeff Gunter and Karen Norbert had worked deep undercover and now their lives were at risk —and their families. The only solution was to find the blackmailer to ensure no sensitive information was ever leaked or printed in the newspapers.

"Where and when is the drop?" Blake watched the clock. Just a little longer...*that's all I need.*

"You'll receive instructions."

Click.

Blake turned and looked at McBride. His face reflected frustration and worry by the deep lines etched across his forehead.

The man shook his head. "Sorry. No go."

Whoever was on the other end of the phone knew the call was being traced. "We need to find this guy, Paul."

"We will. Any news on Whitney?"

Blake looked out the window and had a hard time getting the words out. "Pablo Sanchez took her." He paused for a moment. "Nathan Shaw is involved. Not sure how but he is."

Michelle stopped inside the door. "Sorry to interrupt. The US Marshals are here with your parents and Angel." Her voice cracked with urgency. "They're in your office."

"Okay," Blake said as he watched her turn and leave.

McBride headed to the door. "Jesus. I thought those two pricks were out of your lives for good especially with Shaw's sentencing today. You know I'm here for you. Whatever you need. Just tell me what you want me to do."

Blake had known McBride since Blake and Mike had joined the academy almost eighteen years ago. Paul was a 'brick agent', a rough and tough street agent who had seen it all, from gang violence to the gruesome end results of numerous Las Vegas mob hits. He was a good guy and a good friend. "Thanks. For now, work on figuring out who this blackmailer is. We've got to find him and quick. The ramifications if we don't could turn deadly for Gunter and Norbert. Those confidential files *cannot* be released to the press."

"I'll check with my informants—see what I can find out and also about Whitney."

"I appreciate your help."

"Anytime, my friend. Stay positive. We'll find Whitney."

Blake prayed McBride was telling the truth.

❊ ❊ ❊

Each time Blake looked at Angel he saw his sister, Claire. The same wavy shoulder-length blonde hair and round blue eyes that grinned and sparkled. Their features were identical.

In his office, he sat behind his desk and smiled at the little girl sitting across from him dressed in a powder blue sundress and matching sandals. "Hey. Guess what, Angel? You're going on a mini-vacation with my parents."

Angel cocked her head to one side. "A mini?"

"Yes. Just for a few days."

She shook her head. "I can't. Miss Clarke said we can't miss any school."

"That's okay. I spoke with your teacher and she said you are allowed to miss some classes this week."

Her eyes grew huge and danced with joy. "Really?"

Blake smiled. "Yes. Is that okay with you?"

Angel swung her feet back and forth under the chair and shrugged. "I guess so." With both hands, she picked up the small circular glass paperweight on his desk and pressed her face against it as if looking into a snow globe. "Can we go see Whitney now?"

I wish we could. The thought broke his heart. At least Angel wasn't aware of Whitney's kidnapping. A relief. A bittersweet one. Blake glanced at his parents sitting on the couch.

At sixty-five, his father was still in better physical shape than most men half his age, muscled and lean like a runner.

"Sweetie, Whitney is working out of town right now. You'll see her soon," his mother said as she looked at Blake and wrung her hands in her lap.

Angel set the paperweight down with a thump. Her eyes glossed over. "Why are those men with us?"

Blake detected the hint of panic in her voice. Who could blame her? The poor kid had spent the first three years of her life as a prisoner inside Nathan Shaw's sterile cloning lab at ShawBioGen, endured daily medical testing, was rescued, and then kidnapped by Pablo Sanchez. Not something anyone could get over quickly let alone a child. Blake wasn't sure how much Angel recalled about those days, but judging by her 'highly gifted', level IQ combined with her reaction to the presence of the US Marshals outside the room—she remembered everything.

He didn't like seeing Angel upset and neither did his father. The usually stern marine, now retired, was next to Angel and stroking her hair before Blake was out of his chair. He was surprised by his father's show of compassion and gentleness, something he never experienced while growing up.

"Maybe we can stop and get some ice cream to take on our vacation," his father said.

Brightness and excitement returned to the little girl's eyes. She clasped her hands together. "Can we go now?"

His mother stood and laughed, clearly amused by Angel's impatience.

Angel climbed out of the chair and held her arms out to Blake. He lifted her and hugged her.

She kissed his cheek. "Will I see Whitney soon?"

Thick tension filled the room.

Blake's chest hurt. The torture of not knowing if Whitney was alive was killing him. He set Angel down and forced a smile. "Honey, of course, we will."

❊ ❊ ❊

As the van sped down Interstate 15 toward San Bernardino, Whitney stared at the bloody and bent nail file on the floor.

She would not allow these men to take her to Pablo. She'd fight every step of the way. Injure or kill. Whatever it took to escape.

For the past thirty minutes, she'd been working to pull her feet apart, stretching and loosening the duct tape bound around her ankles until she had finally freed her feet.

Miles ago, Enzo had climbed over the front seat and

was sitting beside his brother with his arm around the man's shoulder.

He glared back at her with black hateful eyes for what she'd done to Raul. Even though his glare sent a shiver down her spine, she felt a twinge of satisfaction.

Enzo lowered his head. His voice quivered. "He's dead —she—killed him." He shaped his fingers like a gun, pointed at her and mouthed, 'you're dead.'

Whitney's hands shook.

The driver glanced in the rear-view mirror, first at her, and then to Enzo. "Lo siento, amigo mío. He was a good man."

Cortez was sorry. That much Whitney understood by the tone of his voice. She looked away, not wanting to admit she felt guilty for what she'd done. Nevertheless, this was survival. Right? What other choice did she have?

For the next half hour, tense silence filled the van until Cortex stopped on the side of the road and shut off the engine.

Why were they stopping?

He exited the vehicle and slid open the passenger side door.

Wind blew through Whitney's hair and for a brief moment she smelled freedom. To where, though? All that surrounded them were boulders, mountains, and desert. There was no place to go. Even if she escaped, she'd die out here. She spotted Cortez's cell phone on the dashboard.

Her chance to contact Blake.

"We can't take Raul with us. It's too risky, Enzo. We must leave him. I'm sorry."

Enzo remained silent as they lifted the dead man out of the van.

"We'll put him over there behind that boulder," Cortez said.

Whitney waited until the men were a safe distance away.

She unsnapped her seatbelt and scooted across the seat. Her feet hit the ground, her body still shaky from the after effects of the chloroform. Keeping her head down she edged along the side of the van and opened the front door just enough to reach the cell phone. She punched in Blake's number and typed in a brief text message.

I-15 Barstow. D Green van. Luv U.

She hit send.

Her pulse pounded as she stared at the screen. Sending...Sending...

Come on. Come on.

Whitney exhaled a sigh of relief when a message popped on the screen confirming the text had been sent. She quickly removed any trace of what she had done and returned the phone to the dash. She was back in her seat with the seatbelt looped over her shoulder seconds before the men returned to the van.

She smiled to herself. *Blake will find me.*

Once Cortez was back in the driver's seat, he turned the ignition.

Enzo stood in front of the open door, still like a statue. His eyes narrowed. "You bitch. You killed him." He snatched her arm and dragged her across the seat.

"Enzo, stop!" Cortez yelled.

"Leave me alone." Whitney smashed her cuffed fists against his arm. The seatbelt slipped off her shoulder.

She heard the engine shut off and Cortez shout, "Let

her go Enzo. Get in the van."

Enzo's eyes were wide and wild with fury.

Whitney knew he wasn't going to stop. He wanted to kill her.

He grunted and yanked her arm until she nearly fell out of the van.

With all her strength, she hit him with a front snap kick to the throat and crushed his Adam's apple. One of the deadliest karate kicks she knew.

His mouth flopped open. His hands instinctively flew around his neck before he toppled backwards. The side of his head bounced off a large rock with a hollow thud like a coconut being cracked open.

She cringed at the stream of blood snaking downhill toward her feet. *I didn't have a choice.* Her head spun and her vision blurred for a second then cleared. Whitney shook her head and stared at Enzo.

He was motionless.

A gun rammed into her side under her ribs.

He clicked the hammer back. "I don't give a shit what Pablo wants. If you flinch—you're dead."

Something was different in his voice. Harshness. Whitney did as instructed. Suddenly, her legs wobbled and she thought she was going to pass out. She gasped for a breath.

She was shrinking.

The world was shrinking.

No. She was falling backwards.

Sleepy. So sleepy...

Blake will find me.

❉ ❉ ❉

In the blazing afternoon sun, Cortez dragged Enzo's

body under the fifty-foot-tall Joshua tree and carefully laid him next to Raul behind the boulder and out of view from the road. Sweat dripped from his forehead and stung his eyes.

Two white-tailed antelope squirrels scurried up the cork-like bark searching for insects to eat.

Cortez wasn't thrilled about leaving the men out in the open, but he couldn't risk taking them to the cargo ship. It would be dangerous enough getting the woman aboard.

Overhead, gigantic vultures squawked and circled. His stomach clenched. He tried not to think about what those birds were going to do to Raul and Enzo's flesh or about the bobcats hiding, waiting to devour their immobile human prey.

He quickly said a silent prayer for the men he'd known since they were kids. "Adiós a mis amigos."

After using a bottle of water from the van to wash the blood from his hands, he lit a cigarette, took a long drag, and contemplated the situation.

A hot arid breeze drifted through his hair and made his scalp tingle. He muttered a curse.

His boss would not be happy. Two of Pablo's best soldiers were dead at the hands of that woman. Cortez had underestimated her.

They all had.

At least she was quiet now. The drugs in her water worked. If he had to keep her drugged until they were in Colombia, he would. He prayed no one had seen the van all over the road earlier and reported it to the authorities. The last thing he needed was another problem. The sooner he got rid of the van the better.

Looking across the Mojave Desert, he pulled the

throw-away cell phone out of his shirt pocket and called Pablo. Every nerve and muscle in his body tensed while he waited for his boss to answer.

"Ho la."

His jaw clenched. "We have a problem."

"What is it, mi hermano?"

Cortez stared at the makeshift burial site of his fallen comrades and took another drag of his cigarette before continuing. "The woman—she killed Enzo and Raul."

Dead silence.

"Where are their bodies?" Pablo asked, anger brewing in his tone.

"I left them in the desert outside of Barstow. I can't take them with us." Cortex swallowed the rock-size lump in his throat and flicked his cigarette to the ground. "I should put a bullet in her head for what she has done—"

"Your chance will come, Cortez. For now. she must be kept alive."

"She won't give us anymore trouble. We'll be in San Diego in less than three hours."

"Be safe. I will see you when you arrive in Colombia."

The call ended.

* * *

Inside his secluded mansion compound overlooking the Bogotá River, Pablo disconnected the call and set the phone on the dresser. His muscles tensed.

The reporter had killed his two best men, and some-one must pay for their deaths.

Ojo por ojo. An eye for an eye.

He walked across the bedroom, the black and white marble floor cold beneath his bare feet. He smiled at the naked brunette sprawled across his king-sized bed, snorting another line of cocaine. On the wall above her hung his favorite original Botero oil painting. Usually, the colorful canvas brought him great joy, but not right now.

Raul and Enzo were dead. Men Pablo had known all his life. Good men. Loyal men. As much as he wanted to, he couldn't order Cortez to kill the reporter. He needed Whitney Steel like a pawn in a chess game to bring Blake directly to him. Then he would slit his throat the same way Blake had slaughtered his twin brother, Manuel, years ago.

Pablo sat on the edge of the bed next to the woman. Her big tits bobbed every time she moved.

She grinned and passed the gold-trimmed glass tray to him. "More?"

He took the tray and snorted two more lines of coke. He sniffed and wiped his nose with the back of his hand. It wasn't long before his body rushed with warm euphoric heat. He felt powerful. Invincible.

Someone has to pay.

He stood and untied the belt of his silk robe and let it the robe fall open. "Come, Bello. Chuparme la polla."

She stared at his erection and ran her tongue across her top lip, delighted by what she saw. They always were.

Whores. The best local whore money could buy, Taliana was stunningly beautiful with the clearest blue eyes he'd ever seen. She'd cost him two thousand US dollars—enough money to keep her dressed in expensive brand-name imported clothing and weekly manicures.

He watched her move off the bed like a slithering snake. She knelt before him.

He shoved his erection into her mouth and closed his eyes, digging his fingers into her shoulders. He tossed his head back and grunted. When he stepped back, he bent forward and kissed the top of her head. Surged clarity filled his head. Pablo wrapped both hands around her neck and lifted her off the floor until her feet dangled.

She kicked at his shins and slapped and tried to claw at his face.

Someone has to pay.

He tightened his grip and squeezed until he heard the last gasp of air escape her lips.

CHAPTER SIX

B lake was breaking apart inside. He couldn't imagine his life without Whitney. He'd never felt so helpless. With a bit of luck, maybe Jerry would be able to provide more details about the men who'd kidnapped her.

Inside University Medical Center, the emergency waiting room was packed to capacity. Blake didn't want to be here. The strong odor of hand sanitizer, stale air and sickness blended together. His hands and feet tingled. Black dots flashed behind his eyes. He blinked a couple times to clear his vision. The last time he had been in a hospital was when Nathan Shaw almost killed him.

He was floating. Fragmented voices and sounds swirled in his head, muffled as if he was under water.

At one point, he'd even thought he'd heard Whitney's voice but couldn't make out what she was saying. Garbled words that didn't make any sense.

Why couldn't he see her?

Rushed footsteps. Commotion. Something poking at his arm.

What the hell was going on? And why did his shoulder and chest hurt like hell? Think. Think. Then he remembered.

Nathan shot him.

Open your eyes.

Bright lights forced them closed.

The faint smell of rubbing alcohol and ammonia.

Dizziness. Queasiness. Crap. The hospital. That's where I am.

He tried to talk. A moan escaped, nothing more. Something was stuck in his throat.

An unfamiliar female voice said, "Dr. Millbank, he's coming to."

Had he been unconscious? God damn it. His chest hurt... heavy, sore and burning.

Blake pried his dry eyes open, blinking, and tried to focus.

"Welcome back," a male voice said.

Apparently, he'd gone somewhere. That didn't sound good. Nope, he didn't want to know.

"You have a tube down your throat. Don't try to talk. Just nod. You're in the recovery room. We had to go in to stop the bleeding. Touch and go there for a bit. But you pulled through just fine. Are you in pain?"

Blake nodded.

The same male voice said, "I'll have the nurse increase your pain medication. There are a couple of people who want to see you."

Whitney. Blake wanted to see Whitney.

He heard Mike's voice first. "Hey, buddy. Damn glad to see you."

Yeah, happy to see you too, man. Glad you're here.

Whitney's face came into focus. She smiled. "I thought I was going to lose you."

I'm not going anywhere. I promise.

He lifted his hand.

Her hand was warm in his. He wanted to say so much. Damn tube. He'd have to wait.

She lowered her head and kissed his cheek. Then her lips

brushed his ear. "I love you. Get some rest."

He held her hand tight. No. Please don't leave. You have no idea how much I love you, honey.

She patted his hand. "Don't worry, we'll have plenty of time when you're back on your feet."

Time. Yes, lots of time. Her hand slipped away...

The swooshing sound of the automatic door brought him back to reality.

He and Mike detoured down a long corridor past the main set of elevators and headed to the recovery room. With every step, the tension increased.

"Hope Jerry's coherent enough to answer some questions."

Blake couldn't agree more. They were slim on leads and needed a break. "The nurse said he was awake but pretty out of it from surgery."

At the end of the hallway, Mike flung open the door to the stairwell. "How are you holding up?"

Not well. Blake climbed the stairs two at a time. "I'll be okay." Panic and fear scraped at his soul. His mind drifted to Nathan Shaw. He glanced at Mike. "Where do you think Sanchez is taking her?"

"Hate to say it but I think he's going to take her out of the country. I doubt he's in the US. Just a feeling."

He knew Mike was probably right. "There are over sixty publicly used, military, and privately-owned airports in Nevada, and that doesn't include former ones no longer in use. If you were a kidnapper, which airport would you use?"

Mike rubbed his chin before he answered. "Hudson or Beatty. Smaller strips with dusk to dawn flights only. Chambers has already alerted all airports to be on the lookout."

The thought made Blake's gut roll with nausea because he knew Whitney could be anywhere. He needed to change the subject before he threw up. "Angel knows something isn't right. She asked about the US Marshals. I hate lying to her."

"She's a smart little girl. Not much gets past her. She'll be fine. I'm sure your parents will keep her busy."

"I'm sure they will. They really love her. Considering my parents' ages, they've really stepped up to help out."

On the third floor, Blake eyed the sign posted at the entrance of the surgical recovery area: *Turn off cell phones and wireless devices.*

That was the last thing he wanted to do. What if Whitney called? Or the blackmailer? He didn't have a choice. He grabbed his phone from his jeans pocket and turned it off.

Outside Jerry's room, a beefy Las Vegas Metro police officer stood guard drinking a coffee.

Blake flashed his FBI credentials.

"Has anyone been in to see him?" Mike asked.

The officer rubbed the back of his neck. "Only his wife. She left about an hour ago. A nurse is in there now."

"Thanks," Blake said before he and Mike entered the room.

While a female nurse dressed in green scrubs changed the bulky gauze bandage wrapped around Jerry's right thigh, Blake paced the recovery area filled with eight surgical patients. Some were awake, others unconscious.

He stared at Mike. His expression was pinched and grim.

Blake knew his chances of finding Whitney were slim. All he had was hope.

When the nurse was done, she peeled off her gloves.

"He's still groggy from the anesthesia and I just gave him some pain medication. We'll be moving him upstairs in a couple of hours."

In the soundproof room, the indirect overhead lighting made Jerry's skin appear pale gray like putty. He had a call bell clutched in his one hand. An IV was inserted in the other.

The camera man raised his head. His eyes widened when he saw Blake. "They—took—Whitney." His voice was full of fear. "I can't believe this happened. This is bad. Real bad."

Blake's stomach muscles tightened. "It's about as bad as it gets." He leaned against the bed's metal side rail. "We don't know where she is, Jerry."

"Oh, God." The cameraman shook his head. "They came out of nowhere. I'm so sorry. I couldn't do anything to help Whitney. I should have tried."

Blake watched the wavy lines peak and dip on the heart monitor. He put his hand on the man's arm. "It's not your fault."

"There was nothing anyone could do," Mike said.

"One minute I was loading equipment. The next thing I knew there was a gun shoved in my face and they had Whitney." Jerry's face contorted in pain and he moaned. "Do you know who took her?"

Blake wasn't sure if he should tell Jerry the truth or not. The man had already been through enough. "We don't know yet. Anything else you can remember?"

Jerry's eyelids grew heavy, and he was clearly fighting to stay awake. "Two of them had a serpent tattoo on their hands. Don't know about the third guy. Right here." He pointed between to his thumb and first finger. "It happened so fast."

His eyes closed.

Before Blake could ask him any more questions, the camera man was snoring loudly.

"Doesn't sound like he knows much more than we do at this point."

"I was praying we'd learn something new. We have to get out of here. I need to check my cell."

Blake switched on his phone the second his feet hit the main floor lobby of the hospital. The phone burst to life, chirping, and beeping, indicating he'd missed calls and text messages. He stopped and looked at the screen. He almost dropped the phone when he read the first message.

I-15 Barstow. D Green van. Luv U.

He exhaled a heavy sigh of relief and turned to Mike. "She's alive."

"Thank God." Mike started to smile then stopped as if he was afraid to get too excited about the news.

After spending fifteen years with the Bureau they both knew things could go south very quickly, and had seen it happen many times.

There would be no excitement until Whitney was safe.

"She's on the Interstate 15 heading toward Barstow in a dark green van. At least she was twenty minutes ago when the text message was sent."

"I'll call Chambers and see if we can get some eyes in the sky right away." Mike grabbed his cell phone from the front pocket of his jeans and made the call.

For the first time, Blake felt as if he was gaining ground and not standing still. Knowing Whitney was alive gave him more hope than anyone could imagine, and he wouldn't stop searching for her until she was safe in his arms.

All he had to do was find her.

✳ ✳ ✳

The late afternoon sun poked through a litter of charcoal gray clouds then vanished as Blake sped the pickup truck down Interstate 15 toward Barstow. Overhead the California Highway Patrol helicopter circled the traffic.

As vehicles zoomed by, he instinctively scanned each one. There had to be thousands of nondescript dark green vans licensed in Nevada and California making the search for Whitney even more difficult.

According to his calculations, they were at least two hours behind her—if the kidnappers were still on the highway and hadn't exited at a turn-off. He tapped his fingertips against the steering wheel, his nerves on edge.

Mike was in the passenger seat talking on his cell phone. By the look of his clenched jaw, the news wasn't good.

Mike ended the call and tossed his phone on the dash. "That was the Barstow Police Department. A hiker discovered two male bodies outside of town. Get this. The locals said the men have tattoos on their hands."

Hope and fear jumbled together. The kidnappers? Had Whitney killed them? She was more than capable. Blake went with his gut. He glanced at Mike, then back to the highway. "She's trying to escape."

"Wouldn't surprise me any. I've seen her in action."

Me too. Blake had witnessed firsthand what she could do to a man twice her size, a man Nathan Shaw had hired to kill her three years ago because she had evidence he'd produced the world's first clone human.

Whitney pointed to a man lying on the living room floor. "Meet the thug who tried to kill me tonight. The police are on their way."

"Tried to kill you? Jesus." Blake bent and checked the man's pulse. He was alive. "You did this to him?"

She nodded. "Would you like me to demonstrate?"

He straightened and glanced at Whitney, who may have weighed a hundred and twenty pounds at best. He then stared in amazement at the two-hundred-pound motionless blob on the floor. "Christ, I think I'll pass."

"My father made sure I could take care of myself. A third-degree black belt in karate. It comes in handy."

"I guess so. I'll have to keep that in mind."

Blake had trained in advanced hand-to-hand combat techniques, but nothing like this woman. Most agents with the Bureau would need a gun, a big gun, to take down a man that size.

Blake rolled down the window part way. Cool air-conditioned air was replaced with a wall of hot, humid air hitting the side of his face. "Let's pray her martial art skills don't backfire and get her killed."

"One thing I've learned about Whitney, she knows to stay calm during a life-threatening situation. Remember Andrew West? She knows when to attack, especially when she has to. We have to have some faith that she'll be okay until we can find her."

Mike was right.

How could Blake forget Andrew West, another low-life Nathan had sent to kill Whitney. West also had his own agenda—revenge for his father's death which had made him a double threat. In fact, Whitney had nothing to do with West's father's death. A suicide. The blame-game hadn't got West anywhere other than dead with a bullet in his head, delivered by Whitney in self-defense.

Mike's cell phone beeped three times. He reached and grabbed the phone from the dash and checked the text message. "We're supposed to meet one of the locals in the parking lot at the Sub Shop on Lenwood."

Ahead, Blake spotted the welcome sign to Barstow. He slowed the truck and exited the highway.

He was familiar with the tourist area since he'd grown up in Las Vegas and recalled many weekend road trips with his friends during his teenage years which also included one secret trip to Hollywood when he was sixteen, even after his parents told him he wasn't allowed to go. Blake was sure his father had known about the "meet the stars" adventure but kept it to himself.

The town looked the same as he remembered. Brightly colored murals adorned the walls of the buildings just off Main Street between 1st and 7th Avenues. Steering the truck onto Lenwood, Blake spied the police car parked in front of the submarine shop. He drove into the lot of the strip plaza and stopped beside the running vehicle. He left the vehicle idling and opened his window all the way.

The guy couldn't have been more than thirty-years-old and had a face shaped like an over-inflated balloon. The uniformed officer rolled down his window.

"Hi. I'm Blake Barnett. This is Mike Jacobs." Blake heard the familiar high-pitched whine of a motor and the distinctive "whump-whump" of rotor blades overhead. His throat tightened. *I have to find her.* The thought played heavy on his mind as the helicopter veered left and swooped southwest toward the coast.

"Justin Perera." He hung his head out the window,

shielded his eyes from the sun, and gawked at the helicopter. He said nothing for a few seconds, then talked in staccato. "The bodies are about a half mile from here." He tossed the police car in drive. "Remember, you're our guests. Follow me."

Just what Blake needed. A rookie cop with an attitude.

Mike finger-combed his hair from his forehead. "Friendly soul."

Blake was thinking the same thing. "Yeah. The usual local hostile welcome."

As he steered the truck out of the parking lot, four sightseers ambled by armed with a map and paraded down the sidewalk lined with hedgehog cactus and yellow flowering creosote bushes. His attention shifted again to the helicopter flying in a wide circle. He fought to keep his hands from trembling.

Two kidnappers down. One to go. Whitney, please be alive...

He turned onto Jasper Road and drove less than a half mile. "Looks like the troops are all here."

Mike undid his seatbelt. "Including Cally. Chambers must have sent him to meet us."

Blake spotted Joe Cally talking to a California Highway Patrol officer. The medical examiner, crime scene techs, and a couple of other familiar faces stood out on the other side of a fence, a few hundred feet from the busy roadway.

He rolled the vehicle to a stop behind Officer Perera's police car and shut off the engine. "Let's see what kind of greeting we get this time around."

"Hopefully, better than the last one."

"Yeah."

Blake never understood the local police's 'you're stepping on my turf' issue. Weren't they all working toward the same end result? In this case—finding Whitney. It used to drive him crazy when he was still a full-time agent. It seemed as if someone was always fighting for the glory.

Outside the temperature hovered in the high nineties, the humidity thick and stifling. The traffic along Lenwood slowed to a crawl as people stopped to gawk, curious as to what was going on.

Blake pushed down the chain-link fence held together with weather-battered wooden posts and climbed over it. The rusted metal links clinked together. Mike followed and almost got the pointed toe of one of his cowboy boots stuck in the fence.

A black and white ground cuckoo bird with short rounded wings strutted by, stopped, scooped up a small rodent then ran.

Mike shook his head. "I can't believe how fast those things go."

"You'd think they'd prefer to fly but they don't." He watched the bird race off in the opposite direction.

As they walked closer to the scene, the hot desert air reeked of fresh blood mixed with raw meat that had been baking in the sun for hours. The odor made Blake's gut churn. After showing their credentials and signing into the scene, Blake and Mike ducked under the yellow plastic police tape. The wind picked up. Tumbleweed scurried across the desert floor. Thunder rumbled in the distance. The faint growl sent the techs scrambling to process any evidence before it could be washed away by the approaching rain.

Joe Cally met them.

"Hey, guys." He looked at Blake and patted him on the back. A small frown formed between his eyes. "How are you doing?"

Frayed nerves were on edge. Blake gazed out over the desert. "I'm okay. I'll be a hell of a lot better when we get Whitney back."

There was a long, silent pause as if Mike and Cally were at a loss for words.

Maybe they were. What do you say to a friend whose fiancée has been kidnapped and might be dead?

Blake shoved his hands in his pockets and watched a female crime scene technician video tape the scene. "Who's in charge?"

Cally grinned. "You're looking at him."

"That's great. Good to see Chambers finally letting you lead an investigation. About time," Mike said.

"I know. Surprised me to. Just to warn you, it looks like a few animals had a go at the bodies. Pretty grisly scene."

As they walked to the towering tree, the stench of decomposing flesh and bodily fluids was overwhelming and sat heavy like a thick fog in the humid air. Four vultures circled overhead and squealed a warning that the corpses belonged to them.

Mike shook his head. "Looks like a wild animal ripped off one their legs. I haven't seen anything like this in a while. Don't really want to see again."

"I'm guessing a bobcat. The limb is still missing." Cally whisked the moisture from his forehead with the back of his hand. "The hiker who found them is pretty shaken up. The locals are getting his statement."

Blake took a few steps and stopped beside a large rock with two cacti next to it.

Blood was everywhere. And feathers.

Between the skin removed from both of the men's faces by the vultures and the gaping hole in one of the men's stomachs exposing muscles and internal organs, Blake was convinced he'd just walked onto a horror movie set. Grisly was an understatement. He moved his focus from the bugs and flies gorging on exposed organs to the small black serpent tattoo on one of the men's hands, confirmation the men were Whitney's kidnappers. "Any word on the cause of death?"

"The medical examiner couldn't tell due to the condition of the bodies. He'll let us know in the morning when he does the post-mortem. He figures they've been dead between two to four hours since there's no sign of lividity, spiders, maggots, or other creepy crawlers." He stopped and took a breath before continuing. "No wallets. No identification. Both men appear to be in their mid-thirties."

The helicopter made another broad pass over the interstate and surrounding area as the ME and his assistant wrapped the corpses in white sheets then placed them in black body bags.

Lightning slashed through the clouds. Thunder boomed. The angry crack echoed Blake's mood.

The frown returned to Cally's face. "I need to talk to the locals and the tech guys before this storm gets worse. I'll call you as soon as I learn anything." He stopped for a moment before continuing. "Hang in there. Whitney's tough. She's going to be okay. We're going to find her."

I hope you're right. A shiver coursed down Blake's spine. "Yeah, we will." Across the hall, Vic and his team were busy trying to uncover clues as to who had hacked into the company's network.

After Cally walked away, Blake's cell phone rang. The shrill sound made him jump. He hoped like hell it wasn't the blackmailer again or bad news about Whitney. He drew a ragged breath and snatched the phone from his shirt pocket.

Large rain drops splattered against his shirt. "Barnett."

"It's Chambers." There was a short airy pause, and then, "A dark green van was spotted by CHP behind Lulu's Kitchen off I15 about forty minutes from you. Might be the vehicle you're looking for."

Blake's hand tightened on the phone. Hope flowed through his veins. "We're on our way. Thanks." He disconnected the call and turned to Mike. "We've got a lead on a van."

The tar-black sky split and rain hammered down.

Mike swiped the rain from his face as they rushed to the truck.

Once inside, Blake slammed the pickup into drive and gunned the accelerator. As he sped down the highway, his mind raced. What if it was too late?

What if Pablo had already killed Whitney?

* * *

Pablo finished snorting another line of cocaine and stared at Taliana lying on the marble floor. Her skin was whitish-gray, her blue eyes wide and cloudy. Purple and red hand imprints bruised her long slender neck. He raised her wrist and unlatched the diamond bracelet he'd given her for her twenty-first birthday and wiped his nose. A shame he had to kill her, but someone had to pay for Raul and Enzo's death. He put on his bathrobe then walked to the bedroom door and opened it.

Eduardo, one of his personal guards, stood outside. Pablo motioned to him to come in the room.

"Get rid of her," Pablo said as he tightened the belt on his silk robe.

Eduardo bent and lifted the woman into his arms. "What do you want me to do with her?"

The woman's skin looked pale against Eduardo's two-tone brown military-style pants and shirt. "Give her to Kato. I'm sure she will be a tasty feast for the cat." At least she was dead and wouldn't feel any pain while the tiger tore her limbs from her body and chewed her up like a fresh kill.

The guard remained silent and slung the woman over his shoulder like a sack of potatoes before heading out of the room and down the hallway.

After he left, Alejandro walked in with a smile on his face and a paper in his hand.

The older man was Pablo's number one associate and close friend who handled day to day operations within the organization as well as running the distribution networks in the US. Over the past twenty-five years, Alejandro had made him a very rich man. Thirty million dollars a day between cocaine and gun sales. Just because Pablo wasn't the head of the cartel anymore didn't mean he didn't continue to reap the benefits. He was once one of the richest men in the world. But he and the cartel took a huge hit when Pablo was arrested and sent to prison. Fifty-five tons of cocaine was seized by various law enforcement agencies during the raid and had cost him and the cartel millions of dollars and—his twin brother's life.

Pablo didn't want to think about how his brother was left to die in a pool of his own blood—his throat slit by the FBI agent. He walked across the room to the bar and poured two glasses of Aguardiente. He handed his associate one and then drank his. The anise-flavored liqueur burned going down his throat.

Alejandro took the ornate crystal glass and downed the liquid in one swallow. He set the glass down on the bar.

"Is everything ready for our guest's arrival?" Pablo peered out the window at the winding river below and then to the bright pink flowers on the Crown of Thorns next to the numerous cacti in the rock garden.

"Yes. The woman's room is prepared. Everything is in place. I've been in contact with our friends at the Policía and their families have been paid off or threatened to ensure they abide by our instructions. This has been circulating in the city as well as in all the villages. Every left-wing group living in the jungle and the mountains will want to collect such a large amount of money."

He handed Pablo a poster with a black and white photograph printed on it.

Pablo stared at the picture.

His right hand tightened into a fist. Anger raced through his limbs at the thought of the man who'd murdered his brother. He would make sure he killed Whitney Steel in front of him exactly the same way Barnett had killed Manuel. He clutched the poster and read the bold red text.

Se Buscan Vivo (Wanted Alive)
Blake Barnett
$US 1,000,000.00

He grinned. "Perfect. Ojo por ojo."

"Manuel would be proud," Alejandro said. "An eye for an eye. The way it should be. The way it has always been."

"Make sure everyone knows I will kill them personally, and their families, if they harm or kill Blake Barnett."

"Of course. I know how important this is to you. You've waited a long time for revenge."

Too long. Pablo stared at Alejandro and noticed how much he'd aged over the past two years after his wife had died from cancer. At sixty-three, his shiny black hair was now completely gray, his skin wrinkled and tanned like dark chocolate due to the hot, unforgiving Colombian sun. "I do have some bad news, Hermano. Raul and Enzo are dead."

The man's brown eyes glassed over. Then his eyes narrowed. "How?"

"Whitney Steel killed them."

The man had been a father figure to Raul, Enzo, Cortez, and Pablo. Life was tough growing up on the streets of Bogotá, and Alejandro always made sure they had food and protected them the best he could. When they were teenagers, he had gotten them odd jobs selling contraband cigarettes and fake IDs. He then helped them move up the ranks within the cartel selling cocaine and weapons.

"I don't understand. How can a woman kill two of our best men?"

Pablo put his hand on Alejandro's shoulder. "Cortez will fill us in with the details when he arrives. In the meantime, the others need to be informed."

"I will do it," the older man said.

"You don't have to."

Alejandro puffed out his chest. He put his hands behind his back. "No. It's my job. I will see to it."

The pain he saw in the man's eyes made Pablo want to rip someone's heart out with his bare hands. "Don't worry. I will make sure Whitney Steel and Blake Barnett both die slowly and painfully. You have my word."

CHAPTER SEVEN

An hour after leaving Enzo and Raul's bodies in the desert, Cortez was relieved to see the orange and white circular logo on the side of the ship supply truck parked behind Lulu's Kitchen, a small truck-stop-style restaurant and gas station off Interstate 15, two hours from San Diego.

He checked his watch. Ten after two. His contact had arrived early.

He glanced at Whitney in the passenger seat, her hair splattered with dried blood. An image of Enzo and Raul's bodies flashed through his mind. The woman would be out cold for at least another six to eight hours, giving him time to get her aboard the cargo ship and begin the week-long voyage to Tumaco. She'd have one nasty headache when she came to, an aftereffect from the Rohypnol Enzo had put in her second bottle of water. Unfortunately, the drug hadn't kicked in quick enough to save Raul.

She looked peaceful, her features relaxed. Not the same woman he witnessed with the devil in her eye who'd brutally killed two of his men, men twice her size. Under normal circumstances, Cortez would have been impressed by her skills. Not this time.

His grip tightened around the steering wheel as he drove into the half-empty lot. Gravel crunched and sprayed up under the tires. After parking behind the restaurant next to the Three Seas Supply truck he shut off the engine.

Reaching into his right sock, Cortez pulled out a roll of hundred-dollar bills secured with an elastic band. He counted out five thousand dollars, money owed to his contact. When he was done, he shoved the remaining cash back into his sock, then got out of the van.

To the southwest, lightning zapped through towering thunderheads along the California coastline.

The driver of the supply truck exited the vehicle and walked to him.

From the information Pablo had provided, his contact's name was Luis Silva. The man appeared to be in his mid-fifties, short and well-fed, his face lined and scarred from a lifetime of acne and hardship.

Silva remained silent and nodded to the back of his truck.

Cortez glanced over his shoulder then followed.

Silva unlatched the metal sliding door of the truck and lifted it open.

Inside were various sized crates loaded with dry goods ready to be delivered to the cargo ship. He spotted the custom built extra wide wooden crate the length of a casket. Just the right size for the woman, with lots of room to spare. Once they were closer to the port they'd transfer her into the container. Between the Customs agents and the San Diego Harbor Police, getting the woman onto the ship would be dangerous, especially with the increased security since 9/11.

Don't think about the risks.

He lit a cigarette and shifted his attention to Silva. "Did you bring enough oxygen?"

"Two tanks just in case," the man said. "Here." He

passed Cortez a short-sleeved navy work shirt with a small triangular Three Seas Supply logo stitched above the left pocket.

Cortez put the shirt on over his T-shirt stained with blood and sweat and buttoned it up. "Do you have the ID?"

The man pulled out a clip-on employee card from his pocket and handed it to him.

After attaching the card to his pocket, Cortez gave him the roll of money.

"Thanks." The man snatched the cash and rammed the bills into the back pocket of his pants. "We need to get moving. The ship leaves at six o'clock."

Cortez checked his watch again. They had less than four hours and they still had a two-hour drive to San Diego. "Help me get the woman loaded."

After pulling out the walk-up ramp, they carried Whitney to the back of the truck and carefully lowered her into the wooden box. Cortez put her purse next to her.

Luis stood back and watched her chest rise and fall. "Are you sure she isn't going to wake up too soon?"

"I'm sure. We'll leave the lid off the crate until we get closer to our destination."

Luis nodded then closed the truck's rear doors and secured them.

"Is everything in place with your contacts at the port?"

"We'll have no problems getting through security. Money talks when you have gambling debts and a mortgage to pay."

He hoped the man was right because Cortez didn't want to disappoint Pablo any more than he already had.

More importantly, he didn't want to get sent to jail like his brother, Alberto. Cortez had a wife and two children to look after. His payment for delivering the woman to Pablo would go toward paying his one son's university education. A medical degree wasn't cheap.

A burst of wind sent dust into a dancing cyclone around the parking lot. Cortez heard the chopper first then spotted it swooping in the distance. He froze when he noticed the blue tail and the letters CHP etched in gold.

I can't get caught.

He opened the back of the van and grabbed his canvas duffel bag. He needed to get rid of his gun. But not here.

He turned and yelled to Silva. "Hurry. We need to get out of here."

❊ ❊ ❊

Blake felt as if his life was falling down around him much like the relentless rain. His heart pounded, and he forced his feet to move. In the distance sirens screamed against the fierce wind, signaling the locals and the crime techs would arrive soon.

The hairs on the back of his neck prickled.

He heeded his internal warning system and inched his way to the green van parked at the back of Lulu's Kitchen.

Please don't be inside dead.

He kept his weapon aimed at the front of the vehicle and thumbed the safety off, his finger on the trigger.

Mike remained two steps behind him with his gun gripped with both hands.

A big rig roared into the parking lot and spit gravel everywhere before stopping at the far end next to the restaurant. Diesel fuel fumes mixed with the odor of deep fried food.

His mouth went dry. Blake glanced over his shoulder and tried to block out the thumping of the helicopter overhead. "I'll take the driver's side."

Mike nodded. He crept to the passenger side of the vehicle, positioned himself at the door, and waited for his cue.

Lightning ignited the sky. Rain slashed at Blake's face and made it difficult for him to see. He rubbed the wetness from his eyes, then flattened his body against the door. He peered through the window and glanced at Mike. "On three." He drew a deep breath and exhaled. "One...two...three..."

At the same time, he and Mike opened the van's doors.

The coppery scent of blood invaded Blake's nostrils. He noticed the large reddish-brown stain on one of the seats. Fear swelled and made his chest ache. He tried not to play scenarios in his head but failed. Did the blood belong to Whitney? Was she dead? Mike's voice cut through his thoughts.

"I know what you're thinking. Let's not panic yet. The blood could be from one of the kidnappers."

Blake lowered his gun and gave himself a moment to breathe. He eyed two empty water bottles splattered with blood, a crumpled paper which appeared to be some sort of a receipt, and a piece of bloodied metal with a narrow leopard print handle. "Check that out." He reached around the seat, careful not to touch anything, and pointed to the floor. "It's Whitney's nail file. Looks like it was used as a weapon." His gut kept telling him she was alive and the thought made him smile inside.

Sirens blared. Red and blue lights flashed and reflected off the van's windows. Two police cruisers and a forensic van sped into the lot.

Mike stepped away from the vehicle and shook the rain from his hair. "There's a lot of low and medium velocity blood splatter on the back of the seat. She may have stabbed one of them or both. We won't know for sure until we get the autopsy reports."

"We've got a bigger problem right now. The kidnapper dumped the van and switched vehicles. We have no idea what the hell we are looking for. He swore under his breath. "For all, we know Whitney could already be out of the country or dead."

Cortez stared out the supply truck's window. The chopper swung west and flew back in the direction of Lulu's Kitchen.

His only goal: get the woman aboard the ship without any complications.

Maybe he was being paranoid. Maybe the police helicopter was looking for someone else, not him. No. Something wasn't right. He dug the throw-away cell phone, one of three he had left, out of his shirt pocket and searched the call and text message log files.

"I think we got out of there just in time. We should be at the port in an hour and a half."

Too close for my comfort. While Cortez examined the call logs, he glanced up at his contact and wondered why Silva would risk his job and possibly his life for a measly five thousand dollars? Probably the same reason he was risking his life—for his family. He shook the thought from his mind and continued to search his phone.

Unable to find any evidence that the woman had made a call, he rummaged through his knapsack and pulled out his gun. He needed to cover his tracks. Pablo would not accept sloppiness. "I have to get rid of the weapon and the cell phone before we get to our destination."

"So far we're ahead of schedule. There's a rest area about ten minutes from here. We can dump them there."

"Good." Cortez stared at the blue digits of the clock on the dash. His stomach growled. "I could use something to eat."

"I'm hungry too and coffee sounds pretty good right now." Silva looked at him, and then back to the traffic ahead. "I know it's none of my business, but what did you give her? She sure looked out of it."

Cortez wasn't in the mood for small talk. Especially reciting particulars about a crime he committed, one which could put him away for life. But he was confident the man would keep any details to himself. If he didn't, he'd have to answer to Pablo, a path no one would want to take.

"Rohypnol. It will keep her out until we are safely on the ship."

"Isn't that some type of date rape drug or something? Heard a lot about it over the years." Silva removed his hat and placed it on the seat beside him.

"It's an effective tranquilizer when needed."

When the blue and white rest area sign came into view, Silva flicked on the turning signal and steered onto the off-ramp. The vehicle hit a pothole and bounced. Coins jumped out of the cup holder and scattered onto the floor. Supplies thudded and clanked in the back of the truck.

"You sure she isn't going to wake up with all that racket?"

"I'm positive. No need to worry." Cortez studied the steady stream of traffic leaving the rest area. "Park over there." He pointed to an open structure with an accordion shaped roof containing a half dozen empty picnic tables that were far enough away from the hustle and bustle of the restaurant and gas station.

Silva stopped and tossed the truck in park. He shut off the engine. "We've got about thirty-five minutes to spare. No longer. We'll have to get something to go. How about pizza?"

Cortez scanned the nearby trees. "Sure. You go ahead. I'm going to ditch these." He held up the gun and cell phone. "Meet you inside the restaurant."

Silva nodded and got out of the truck.

Clutching the weapon, magazine, and cell phone, Cortez exited the vehicle and shut the door. The wind had calmed and the raging rain had slowed to an intermittent light drizzle. He hurried to the tree line out of the view of incoming headlights. With each step water swooshed and sucked under his shoes from the earlier downpour. He threw the items as far as he could. He heard rustling like crunching leaves, followed by a thud as each of the items hit the ground.

When he turned, a police cruiser drove slowly up beside the supply truck, too slowly, as if the driver was inspecting the vehicle.

Cortez couldn't move for a second and then skirted behind the picnic structure. He poked his head around the corner and watched. The cop car inched forward then stopped for what seemed like forever. Brake lights finally vanished toward the gas station. He breathed a sigh of relief and ran back to the truck, his appetite evaporating by the second. He couldn't take the chance and check on the woman. Not here. Not with the police snooping around.

He decided to wait in the truck instead of meeting Silva inside the restaurant—in case the cop came around again. Cortez didn't want or need any more problems. Two dead men were enough.

CHAPTER EIGHT

As the afternoon gloom shifted into evening darkness, the rain was a distant memory but not the events of the day. Blake couldn't shake the horrified look on Whitney's face from of his mind. He had no idea where she was—no idea where to look.

Back at the office, his stomach was doing flip-flops even though on the exterior he appeared as calm as he possibly could under the circumstances. A part of him was terrified he might lose Whitney. That was the reality, and right now reality sucked.

He had to find her. Failure was not an option.

Across the hall, Vic and his team were busy trying to uncover clues as to who had hacked into company's network. It wouldn't be long before Blake would have to deal with the blackmailer.

He looked at Mike sitting across the desk from him. "Can you check and see if those DNA results are in yet on the cigarette butts found at the courthouse? It might help if we at least know who we are looking for."

"I'll call Chambers and see if we have an ID yet. You know—you can't live on that stuff." Mike stood and pointed to the cup of coffee in Blake's hand. "I think I'll slip out and grab us something to eat."

Blake sunk into the chair and looked at his cup of lukewarm coffee, number eight, six more than he usually drank. He knew better than anyone he needed to keep up his strength. He had to stay strong for Whitney. "You're right. I could use a burger."

"Okay. You got it. I'll be back in a bit."

After Mike left, Blake leaned his elbows on the desk and rubbed his temples. He wondered what he would tell Angel if anything happened to Whitney. The thought made his chest squeeze. He needed to stay positive but he knew from years with the Bureau, the first forty-eight hours were the most crucial especially when searching for a missing person. It had been almost twelve hours since Whitney was abducted.

His cell phone rang. He grabbed his phone from the desk and answered the call. "Hello."

"A collect call from Nathan Shaw. Will you accept the charges?" a female voice asked.

He snapped the pen he had in his hand in half. "Yes."

"Go ahead," the operator said.

The muscles in Blake's arms tensed. "What the hell do you want?"

"Any luck finding our lovely Miss Steel?"

The nasal tone of Nathan's voice sent ripples of rage zooming through him. "You know damn well I don't know where she is. No thanks to you."

"Ah, Blake. I have nothing to do with Miss Steel's disappearance. It's too bad Mr. Kurtz wasn't willing to take my more than fair deal earlier today. If he had, you would know exactly where your fiancée was and right now you would be at home enjoying each other's company."

"Piss off." His voice grew louder. "Stop contacting me or I'll get a restraining order."

"Remember." A long pause. "I am the *only* one who knows where she is right now. Maybe we could make a different deal, one which would benefit both of—"

Blake disconnected the call. He didn't have a choice. Regardless of what Shaw wanted, Blake couldn't give it to him. It wasn't his call. Only Jason Kurtz or the Justice Department could make those types of decisions and Shaw was perfectly aware of that fact. It was clear the call was nothing more than a twisted sick taunt from a desperate killer who would soon be executed. That day couldn't come fast enough.

"Is everything okay?"

Blake swiveled in the chair and looked up to see Vic in the doorway. "Yeah, I'm fine. Just a bit stressed."

"That's understandable. Any news on Whitney?"

"Not yet." He wished there was news. "How are things going on your end?"

"We've retrieved the full IP address. The intruder used a proxy server to gain access to the network—meaning they could have bounced their activity off a system anywhere in the world. We're working on a warrant to examine the service provider's records to determine who used the IP address at the time of the illegal activity." Vic slid his hands into his pant pockets before continuing. "Once we have the records, Hamlin will do what we call a traffic analysis. It should provide us with more information. Like I said it's slow going. Wish I had better news. The reality is there is no way we're going to know who's responsible before the deadline tomorrow."

This was the last thing Blake needed to hear. Without knowing who he was dealing with, he had no choice but to meet the blackmailer tomorrow when he needed to be focused on Whitney. Then it hit him. And he didn't like where this was going. "Jesus. What if that was the plan all along?"

Vic raised an eyebrow and stared at him with a blank look on his face. "What do you mean?"

"What if the blackmail attempt is nothing more than a ploy to distract me from finding Whitney? What if the hacker has no intention of releasing those files to the press?"

"You might be right. But can you afford to take that chance?"

Could he? Agents' lives were at stake. What if he was wrong? Blake stood and walked to the window. He cracked his knuckles. "I don't know. My gut keeps telling me everything that's happened today is connected. I'm just not sure which one is the puppet-master—Nathan Shaw or Pablo Sanchez."

❉ ❉ ❉

After downing three pieces of pizza, Cortez finished the last of his coffee and dropped the empty Styrofoam cup onto the floor next to the growing collection of discarded fast food containers. "We need to stop soon. I have to check on the woman and get her ready."

They'd passed the sign to the San Diego Zoo almost a half hour ago. He thought about his kids and how they'd never been to a zoo before. Maybe after this job was finished he would bring his family here. His wife would enjoy the trip. She worked hard at the restaurant morning until night. She deserved a vacation. They all did.

"No problem." Silva lit a cigarette and rolled down his window.

Salty ocean air filled the cab of the truck. Headlights flickered and glared off the dirty windshield.

"We'll be hitting the outskirts of San Diego in a few minutes."

As they approached the city, Cortez's stomach knotted in a hard ball like a rock. "You sure you can trust your person at the port?"

"Sure can. He's my brother-in-law—a harbor cop. Been one for six years now. Hey, if you can't trust family. Who can you trust? Your boss uses us on a regular basis to help distribute his products." Silva looked at him then back to the road. "Most people don't realize that the US-Mexican border is only twenty-five miles from the port. Quite handy for gun runs."

A cop? That new revelation didn't make Cortez feel any better. He was taking a huge risk as it was. Whether he liked it or not, he had to believe the man sitting across from him. Besides, Pablo would never involve people he didn't trust with a job so important.

"There's an empty lot ahead." Silva pointed out the window. "Next to the gas station." He steered into the area and parked away from the road under a street light.

After shutting off the truck, Cortez pulled out two lengths of clear flexible tubing and a roll of tape from of his backpack. He undid his seatbelt and opened the door.

Silva climbed out of the driver's seat and closed the door.

Cortez waited at the back of the vehicle and scanned the gas station as Silva unlatched the heavy metal sliding door and pushed it up. He yanked out the walk-up ramp and headed inside. He was relieved to see the woman was in the exact position he'd left her in.

"She's snoring pretty damn good. Louder than I do." Silva chuckled.

She was alive. That's all that mattered. He bent and slipped his arms under the woman's shoulders. "Give me a hand."

Silva grabbed her feet and they lifted her out of the box and placed her on the floor. Silva handed him one of the portable oxygen tanks.

Cortez secured a length of tubing to the end and deposited the tank inside the crate. He slowly turned the flow control valve and watched the needles on the dual gauges move. The tank hissed.

"You want the other one?"

"Yes. I don't want to take any chances. If one fails she could suffocate." If anything happened to the woman before he got her to Pablo, his boss would not be happy with him.

After assembling and testing the second tank, Cortez taped the tubing directly below Whitney's nostrils to ensure she would get enough air. When done, they lifted her back into the box and stuffed her belongings inside. He then set the crate's lid on top and camouflaged the chest with containers of dry goods to help muffle the sound of the running tanks. At least now no one would know about the woman, and transferring her to the ship should be much easier and safer. He turned to Silva. "We're set."

As they drove toward the port, airplanes flew in and out of the San Diego International airport; their tail lights blinked and looked like shooting stars trailing across the clear night sky. Their engines whined and roared over the open water. The sound was unnerving and reminded Cortez of the police helicopter at Lulu's Kitchen.

Silva turned on the interior light in the cab and reached overhead and opened the glove box. He passed him a folded paper then shut off the light. "The ship you'll be on is small but much faster than most—a feeder. They're used to transfer cargo between ships and smaller-scale ports. It will get you to your destination in half the time."

Four days sounded much better than eight at sea. Cortez took the paper and put it in his shirt pocket. "Thanks. I appreciate your help. I am sure my boss will reward you and your brother-in-law for a job well done."

Regardless of how deadly Pablo could be, and Cortez had seen him in action many times, his boss always made sure his 'family' was looked after.

"Don't thank me yet. Not until you're aboard the ship."

Cortez peered through the window and spotted the blue and white Port of San Diego sign approaching on the right. He sat forward in the seat. He didn't feel comfortable not having a gun in case something went wrong. He riffled through his knapsack and located his silver spring-loaded switchblade, a gift from Pablo when they lived on the streets, and slid it in the back pocket of his jeans.

"My brother-in-law will meet us at the 10th Avenue terminal."

He lit a cigarette, took a long drag, and blew the smoke out the window. Cortez would be glad once he had the woman on the ship and they were en route to Tumaco.

Silva slowed the truck a few yards away from the terminal's security check-in station. He lowered his window all the way. "Just act natural. Like you've done this a dozen times."

Cortez nodded then flicked what was left of his cigarette out the window. They'd be setting sail soon. His hands were clammy and damp. He wiped them over the knees of his jeans and tried to relax. As they drove closer,

Cortez noticed the Harbor Police patch on the man's black shirt.

"Jack said you'd be around. Kind of a late delivery for you," the officer said.

Silva scooped a stack of paperwork from the dash and handed it to the man. "Yeah. Not my usual run. Gotta make sure the *TransVenture* has everything they need before they leave. Don't want the crew running out of coffee or sugar halfway through the trip."

The man laughed and then thumbed through the paperwork. "You know the drill."

The metal arm of the gate raised and Silva drove forward a couple of yards and rolled to a stop.

"What's going on?" Cortez reached into his back pocket and pulled out his switchblade.

Silva held up his hand. "No need for that. He's got to check the cargo. Stay cool. And put that thing away."

Cortez undid his seatbelt and watched in the side-view mirror as he clutched the knife in his hand. He heard the back door of the truck grind open.

If the woman was discovered, he would be forced to kill the police officer. Not something he wanted to do.

He listened to the muffled voices, unable to make out what Silva and the officer were saying. All he could do was wait, his eyes shifting back and forth to the clock on the dash and the side-view mirror. Five long minutes passed. He heard the back door of the truck slide down with a loud bang. Cortez breathed a sigh of relief.

"Have a good night," the officer said.

Silva opened the door and hopped into the driver's seat. "All done. Should be smooth sailing from here."

"I hope you're right."

The man steered the supply truck onto Harbor Drive.

The port's lights merged with the lights from the city and glistened a rainbow of colors off the calm water.

Silva stopped the truck and shut it off.

Two men stood in front of the *TransVenture II* smoking cigarettes. The men looked tiny compared to the massive blue and gray colored ship.

"Those are the guys you can trust. They'll help you get your package aboard. Oh, there's Jack. Right on time." Silva took off his ball cap and wiped the sweat from his forehead with his hand before putting the hat back on.

He observed a tall man with a bald head dressed in a black police uniform shirt and pants stalk his way toward the supply truck. Cortez slipped his knife back in his pocket then got out.

Silva jumped out of the vehicle and greeted his brother-in-law with a hug. "Hey man. Haven't seen you in a few weeks."

"Good to see you, man. We're going to have to get together for a few beers real soon." The man smiled then turned to Cortez. "You need to hurry. The Customs and Border Protection guys make their rounds with the dogs in less than forty-five minutes."

"Let's go. The last thing we need is to get caught," Silva said. He turned and hurried to the back of the truck. His bother-in-law waved to the other men to join him.

❋ ❋ ❋

Twenty-five minutes later, Cortez was aboard the ship in a secluded room away from the crew with his precious cargo. Pablo's cargo. After removing the lid from the wooden crate, he reached in and shut off the oxygen tanks. He stared at the woman sleeping peacefully and knew he couldn't leave her in the box. No way. Not after what she'd done to Enzo and Raul. Sadness gripped his thoughts at the loss of his friends killed by Pablo's prize.

Cortez shook the thoughts from his mind and picked up Whitney's purse. He dumped the contents on the bed. He picked through the items and removed anything that she could use as a weapon. Pens, cosmetic mirror, and a hair brush. He wasn't taking any chances after witnessing what she could do to two grown men.

Afterward, he slid both arms under her neck and knees, lifted her out of the crate, and gently placed her limp body on the bed. He rolled her on her side in case she woke and got sick from the drug he'd put in her water. Next, he dug through his knapsack and pulled out the handcuffs Silva's brother-in-law had given him. Cortez put one handcuff around Whitney's right wrist, clicked it closed, and attached the other cuff to the metal frame of the bed.

In four days they would be in Tumaco and then on their way to Pablo. Cortez sat on the edge of the bed and looked at the woman. He smiled to himself, satisfied.

Whitney Steel wasn't going anywhere.

❉ ❉ ❉

Mike returned with two double burgers, fries, and two colas. As much as Blake didn't feel like eating, he had to. It was going to be a long night.

"Good news and bad news. I talked to the lab. You won't believe this. The DNA on one of the cigarette butts belongs to Cortez Guerrero, Alberto's brother."

Pablo Sanchez's cousin. Blake gulped hard, forcing down the partially chewed chunk of meat that had lodged in his throat. Finally, able to swallow, he set his burger down and digested the news, remembering the night he gave the order to shoot Alberto after Pablo Sanchez had kidnapped Angel.

Sanchez's face twisted. He took a few steps backwards and waved toward the van.

The side van door opened. His cousin, Alberto, jumped out. He grabbed Angel and lifted her out and placed her on the ground beside him. He kept his hand on her shoulder.

Please don't move, Angel.

Blake prayed Mike was ready. He'd only have one chance.

"Take Alberto out," Blake whispered.

He held his breath and waited.

"See, she is well. Now we trade." Pablo stepped forward.

Take the shot.

"Sure." Blake was not getting Whitney out of the car no matter what.

Come on. Shoot, Mike.

Blake heard the rifle fire. The shot hit Alberto square in the stomach. He doubled over, fell to one knee, and then crumpled to the ground...

Voices drifted from across the hall and nudged him back to the conversation. "|It appears that Cortez is picking up the slack while his brother's in prison."

"I'd say so. Let's pay Alberto a visit first thing in the morning, feel him out and see if he knows anything about his brother's whereabouts and Whitney."

"Definitely." A long beat of silence passed before Blake spoke again. "What do we know about Cortez?" He picked up his burger and took a few bites before setting it down again.

"He's got a rap sheet. Mainly petty crap when he was seventeen. Selling weed, shoplifting, graffiti. Nothing as an adult. He's forty-four, married, two adult kids." Mike took a long sip of his cola and then continued. "He's owned a small restaurant over on Warm Springs Road for the past twenty-five years."

"To everyone else, he's basically a law-abiding citizen who appears to have a normal and respectable life except for the fact he works for a top Colombian drug lord, Pablo Sanchez."

"Exactly."

After Blake finished his dinner, he tossed the wrappers into the pail beside his desk. He slouched back in the chair. "I hate sitting here doing nothing. The waiting is killing me."

"We've got a lot of eyes out there looking for her. Man, we are going to find her. We'll scoop up Cortez's wife and see if we can squeeze something out of her. I don't think there's any reason to talk to Alberto. The guy isn't going to rat out his brother."

Blake rubbed the back of his neck and tried not to focus on his aching muscles. Fatigue and stress were playing havoc with every part of his body. They still had another problem. "What the hell are we going to do about the blackmailer? I spoke with Vic earlier. He said there's no chance we'll have an ID on this guy before the deadline tomorrow."

Mike shook his head. "Shit." His brows furrowed as he shoved the last fry in his mouth and chewed. "I was hoping the team had discovered something usable by now."

"You and me both. We have to go on the assumption the meet is going to happen. I'll play the game. But there is no way this person is getting one cent from me, let alone a million bucks."

"Man, I hear you. I'll setup some backup so we can nab the bastard. I'm positive Cally and McBride will want to help."

"Thanks. I appreciate everything you and the guys are doing—including Chambers. I'm thankful for the support."

Mike rolled his chair away from the desk and stretched his legs. He folded his arms across his chest. "Rambo Robot has surprised all of us, which in this case is a good thing."

Blake couldn't help but smile at Mike's nickname for their former SAC. Regardless of how they both felt about Trent Chambers, the man had stepped up offering any of the Bureau's resources and manpower to assist in finding Whitney. For that, Blake would be forever grateful. He lowered his head and stared at the paperweight on his desk. His gut gnarled and churned, and not from the meal he just ate. Panic bubbled up again. The unknown. Worry. Missing Whitney. He needed to do something. Needed to stay busy.

While Mike finished his burger, Blake flipped open his laptop and brought up a detailed map of California. He stared at the junction of highways running through Barstow where the kidnapper's remains were discovered. He marked major and private airports, train and bus stations. He let out a heavy sigh. "Any idea when we'll have IDs on the two kidnappers?"

Mike balled up the paper wrapper from his burger with one hand and did an overhead basketball-type toss into the waste can. "Chambers has a rush on it. We should have something by mid-morning."

"Good." Blake reached and turned his laptop sideways so Mike could see the screen. "If we go on the assumption that the kidnapper is trying to get Whitney out of the country there are only a few ways to do that based on the location where the bodies were dumped. Air or boat. We know Whitney hasn't been spotted at any of the airports. My gut's telling me they were on Interstate 15 for a reason. At any time, they could have taken another route." He ran his finger down the screen and pointed. "Which leads us here and here."

"San Diego or Los Angeles. Best theory we've got so far. How though? With security tighter than ever at both ports, it would be difficult to wander around with a kidnapped woman without anyone noticing. Whitney would be kicking and screaming."

"You're right about that. She'd be fighting every step of the way. That's the part I don't know. The how." Blake reclined back in the chair and cracked his knuckles. "Or which port." His mind drifted in a dozen different directions then back to one question. "What if I'm wrong?"

"Man, stop second guessing yourself. As long as I've known you your gut has never been wrong."

Why *was* he questioning himself? Because this time was different. The crime was too close to home and one wrong decision could put Whitney's life in jeopardy if it hadn't already. "You're right again." He drew a deep breath and exhaled. "Okay. Where do we go from here? San Diego or Los Angeles."

"Well—" The office phone rang and interrupted Mike.

Aware Michelle had already left for the day, Blake picked up the receiver. "SecuraCorp."

"Tomorrow."

Blake recognized the digitized disguised voice. He held his hand over the mouth piece, turned to Mike and mouthed, *blackmailer*.

Mike sprang out of the chair and rushed out the door to the conference room where Vic and his team were still working.

"Three thirty at Freedom Park," the voice said on the other end of the call.

A long pause then a high-pitched hiss.

"Put one hundred packets of ten thousand dollars secured with elastic bands in a small black bag. No SecurityPac. Drop the bag inside the green garbage can at the west entrance next to the swimming pool. If my instructions aren't followed exactly, I will leak the information regarding numerous covert FBI operations, including the real names and addresses of the undercover agents involved, to the press as well as post the details on the Internet."

Blake fixated on the second hand of the wall clock. He needed to keep the conversation going long enough to get a trace.

"How do I know we aren't going to do this dance again in a week or a month? I mean seriously. You claim you have the information so what's stopping you from demanding more money down the road?"

"Come alone. No cops. Understand?"

"Perfectly. You didn't answer—"

The call ended with a click and then a dial tone.

Mike walked back into the office shaking his head. "No go." He scratched his chin. "Is it just me or do you think it's a bit odd he used the word SecurityPac and not dye pack? The average Joe wouldn't even know that."

Blake nodded. "Also sounded as if he was reading from a script. Like I said to Vic, I have a feeling this little game is nothing more than some twisted tactical manoeuvre to keep me distracted long enough so the kidnapper can get Whitney out of the country with or without Sanchez along for the ride. Let's hope to God I'm wrong because we both know our odds of finding her drop the second she's out of the US."

❋ ❋ ❋

Whitney licked her dry lips and moaned. Her mouth tasted like she'd been sucking on a penny wrapped in tin foil drenched with some type of floor cleaner. Her head hurt like hell. It felt as if something had been drilling into the back of her skull or she'd been hit hard. She cringed. The pain was agonizing. Was she hurt? Bile inched up her throat. She forced it down then inhaled and exhaled deeply through her nose over and over until the nausea finally disappeared.

Lifting her hand, she searched the back of her head for an injury. There wasn't any. No bumps or cuts. Whitney pried her eyes open. Darkness greeted her along with the strong odor of fish and tangy salt air.

Then came panic.

After rolling flat on her back, she tried to prop herself up on her elbows but her right wrist was caught on something. She yanked her arm hoping to free it. When metal clanked against metal, Whitney realized she was handcuffed. With her left hand, she felt around blindly. From what she could tell she was lying on cloth. Maybe blankets. Maybe on a bed or a couch. But where was she?

Damn it. Why couldn't she remember what happened?

Panic rippled up again. "Help me." Her voice came out as a muted squeak. She tried again. This time she yelled. "Help!"

Heavy footsteps.

A door opened.

Light blinded her. She turned her head away from the

brightness then slowly back.

"You're awake," a man said as he closed the door leaving it cracked open an inch.

The voice was familiar. Whitney couldn't place it. She searched her foggy mind for answers and fought through a haze of confusion. The courthouse. A van. Then she remembered more.

Kidnappers. Blood...

She turned toward the voice and squinted. The outline of a man's face came into focus. She sucked in a hard breath. *Cortez.*

"You need to drink." He handed her a bottle of water. "You're dehydrated. You'll feel better once you get enough fluids into you. Drink slowly or you'll be sick."

Whitney ran her tongue over her parched lips and grasped the bottle. She took a sip and swallowed. The cold water felt good against her throat but didn't wash away the horrid taste in her mouth. She took another drink and couldn't believe how heavy and weak her muscles felt. It took all her strength to hold the bottle. What happened to her? She licked her lips again. "What did you do to me?"

"I did what I needed to do—to get you here."

"Where is here?"

"Are you hungry? I'll have the crew cook you something. You'll need to regain your strength."

"Crew?" Her body shook and her voice grew louder. "Where the hell am I?"

"On a cargo ship to Tumaco, Colombia."

Dear God. He was taking her out of the US and into Pablo's hands—hands that wanted to kill her. Terror clawed through her veins and she tried to control her fingers from trembling. She thought about Blake and how much she loved him. She glanced at her diamond engagement ring and wanted to cry. *Keep it together. Don't let him defeat you.* She had to remain calm. Her life depended on it. And her future.

Cortez set two red sweat shirts and pants, two pairs of socks, and a pair of canvas running shoes on the bed. "Get changed."

She heard a distinctive click and saw the shiny blade of a switchblade in the diffused lighting.

He walked behind her and removed the handcuff from her wrist.

She flinched.

"If you try anything like you did with Enzo and Raul, I'll slice you from ear to ear, and when I'm done I'll kill someone you care about. Perhaps the little girl."

He knows about Angel. No. How could he?

Cold steel touched her throat and pressed tight below her chin almost cutting the skin.

Every muscle in Whitney's body froze.

"You killed my friends. That's not something I'm going to forget."

CHAPTER NINE

Whitney exhaled the breath she was holding as soon as Cortez closed and locked the door. Her hands were still shaking. If the man had the chance he'd make good on his threat to kill Angel, especially after she'd killed Raul and Enzo. The thought terrified her. She prayed Blake had the little girl hidden somewhere safe.

Determined to find a light, Whitney stumbled about the dark room, groping and bumping into things, her limbs weak and tired. Clearly, Cortez had drugged her—with what, she didn't know. She doubted he'd freely reveal that information. He'd already dodged the majority of her questions.

After locating a table lamp, she flicked it on. The air-conditioned space looked like much like a hotel room decorated in muted shades of green and dark wood complete with a double-wide lounge chair, small sofa, built-in desk, bed, and a mini bar fridge. Next to the cupboards was a space that appeared to have once housed a room to ship telephone.

But this wasn't a hotel room at an exotic resort or spa.

It was a floating prison.

The realization hit her hard and she wanted to scream. But didn't.

She was stuck in this cabin, a prisoner, with no place

to go—no way to escape. Every decision she made from here on out would determine not only if she lived or died but also the fate of a little girl that she loved. Whitney shook the horrifying thought from her mind and glanced at her surroundings, her new home　for God knows how long.

She was aware that people took vacations on freight-type vessels instead of sailing by passenger cruise ships and she never understood the fascination. From what Whitney had read, this type of travel was more about the journey than the final destination. Not for her. It was more about her final destination than the journey. Colombia. To Pablo. A chill ripped up her spine.

Maybe it was a traveler's need to get away from technology. It sure wasn't for the peace and quiet—the constant creaking noise, low humming, and the vibration coming from the engine and the containers above shifting on the surface of the ship. Steel grinding against steel.

There was no television or radio and she didn't know if the ship had Internet. Just because she didn't have it in the cabin didn't mean it wasn't available. She was positive her captor had carefully removed any links to the outside world specifically for her.

Whitney spied the collection of a dozen paperbacks on a shelf beside the desk, their spines cracked and scratched, worn from years of overuse. Most of the books were in Spanish and the three English ones were predominantly for men. A deck of playing cards lay on an oak coffee table in front of the sofa next to an outdated copy of *Time* magazine.

She went to the refrigerator and pulled the door open. Inside she found six bottles of water and a tray of sliced pineapple, strawberries, and mango. Her stomach growled and reminded her Cortez would be back soon with something else for her to eat. The thought of the man returning sent a chill through her body. Right now, she'd do anything to have Blake's arms wrapped around her, to be home. To be safe.

Before heading to the cramped bathroom to shower and change into the clean clothes provided for her, Whitney plunked down on the bed and searched her purse for something she could use as a weapon. Cortez had removed anything sharp including her pens, makeup mirror, and even hairbrush. She unzipped the interior side pocket of the purse and realized he had removed her epinephrine autoinjector. Having a severe allergy to shellfish and being held against her will on a boat didn't go well together. Whitney needed to get it back.

She tossed the contents back into the bag. How dare he threaten her by using Angel. Wasn't it enough he'd kidnapped her for Pablo Sanchez, that he would be an ac-complice in her impending demise?

Anger blasted through her. Threats or no threats. Whitney had never backed down from anything in her life and this time was no different.

Even if she used her karate skills to kill her captor, what about the ship's crew? How many were there? How many passengers were on board? Could she get to the ship's radio and call for help? So many unknowns.

The 'unknowns' outweighed her desire to live—to marry Blake and adopt Angel. A life Whitney wanted to begin.

First, she had to regain her strength. Then she needed to come up with a plan to save her life.

Whitney's eyes pleaded with Blake to help her. She kicked

repeatedly at the kidnapper, her strength fading by the second.

The kidnapper looked at the camera and laughed. In slow motion, he pulled a gun out from his jacket and pressed the barrel against her temple. He looked at Blake and slowly smiled. Then he pulled the trigger...

Blake jolted upright, gasping. "Jesus."

His skin was slick with perspiration. An icy chill ran through his veins. It took a few seconds for him to get his bearings and realize he was at home, in his bedroom—his and Whitney's bedroom.

It was only a dream. A bad dream he needed to shake from his mind but couldn't. The look on Whitney's face...

I should have been there to protect you.

Blake drew a deep breath and looked at the neon blue numbers on the digital clock on the nightstand. It was almost one o'clock in the morning, and he'd been asleep for less than an hour. He snatched his cell phone from the nightstand and checked to make sure he hadn't missed any messages. Nothing. He laid back down and stared at the ceiling. The light hum of the fan was the only sound he heard. It was too damn quiet in the house.

No Whitney. No Angel.

After tossing off the sheets, he sat on the edge of the bed with his elbows resting on his knees, his hands steepled. The damn dream had him spooked. He needed to get out of here and go for a drive. The last thing he wanted to do was sleep, at least not right now. In the light filtering through the corners of the blinds from the streetlights, he pulled on a T-shirt and jeans. When he was done dressing, he ran his fingers through his hair and grabbed his keys.

❊ ❊ ❊

Blake parked the pickup across from the safe house on Harmon Avenue and shut off the ignition. He looked at the house, not sure why he was here.

The US Marshal's black sedan was parked two houses up obscured by tall bushes. Matt Thompson and Terry Price were good guys. Trusted guys who'd been with the Marshall Service for over twenty years. Blake was confident the two men would keep Angel and his parents safe.

A silver four-door compact car was parked in the driveway—a dummy vehicle to make things appear more legit in the working-class neighborhood.

A dog barked in the distance.

A horn honked.

The hairs on the back of his neck stood at attention.

He straightened in the seat and hung his head out the truck's window and looked up and down the street. No one. Only wavy shadows from the overhanging trees and streetlights strolled the sidewalks of the dead-end street. He never liked this neighborhood, especially for a safe house. Too suburban. Too populated. Too many back yards for bad guys to hide in.

The front door of the fire-proof constructed two-storey home was painted a dark golden brown and contained steel plates and a fully bolstered steel frame. The windows were fitted with bulletproof Plexiglass. Certainly not fail-proof, but they would at least buy some time to get to safety.

The FBI had purchased the two nondescript bungalows on either side which were rented to employees at the Bureau. The added security gave Blake a little more comfort knowing there were extra agents next door.

He spied the satellite dish on the roof used for back up communications. No way could anyone get into the house undetected. Between the state-of-art security system providing real-time information on intruder sounds and locations, concealed interior and exterior motion sensors and cameras, it would take an army to bust in and by that time his parents and Angel would be safe and secure in the metal encased panic room.

Then why was he here? Everything was fine. Everyone safe.

He checked his watch. One forty-five in the morning. It wasn't as if his parents or Angel would be awake. There weren't any lights on in the house except for a dim light coming from the den on the main floor—a light that was always left on via a timer.

Blake tried to ignore the fear gnawing at his gut. He knew all too well that his chance of finding Whitney was remote as each hour came and went. He'd do anything to hear her voice. To smell her hair. More than anything he prayed he wouldn't have to bring her home in a body bag.

Shooing away the troubling thought, he turned the key in the ignition and started the truck. His cell phone rang. He stopped the pickup, grabbed his phone from the passenger seat, and checked the caller ID. It was Hal. "Hey man."

"Where are you?"

"On Harmon at the safe house. I'm just leaving."

"I think I've got something. Meet me at the coffee shop on Flamingo in fifteen."

Fear disappeared and was replaced by a small amount of hope. Maybe he would find Whitney before it was too late. Blake peered in the rear-view mirror and watched a set of headlights approaching quickly behind him. "On my way."

✳ ✳ ✳

Cortez bent and set the tray containing cheese, crackers, scrambled eggs, and plastic cutlery on the table in front of the lounge chair. "You need to eat. We have a long trip ahead of us."

Whitney stood in the corner of the room next to the small desk with her hands on her hips. Her hair was still wet from the shower and fell in waves across her shoulders. The color had returned to her face, her cheeks soft pink under the glow of the desk lamp. She'd changed into the clothes he'd brought her. The sweat suit appeared a bit too large but still clung to her body. Beautiful yet deadly. It was too bad that Pablo would probably kill her.

"Give me back my EpiPen right now. I'm allergic to shellfish. For God sakes, we're on a boat. What if I have a reaction?"

She was right. Pablo would not be happy if anything happened to her. But Cortez knew the woman was resourceful. He'd witnessed the way she used her nail file to kill Raul. If he handed over the pen she could easily use it on him as a weapon. A shot of adrenaline could put him at a huge disadvantage or maybe even kill him.

He couldn't leave the pen with her. He'd have to come up with another solution.

"After what you did to Raul and Enzo, I will stay here with you and handcuff you to the bed at night for my own safety. That way you will get the medication if you have a reaction."

Her eyes narrowed and her hands balled into fists at her side. She wasn't happy about the idea. Neither was Cortez. He'd be forced to sleep with one eye open to make sure she didn't discover a way to try to murder him while he slept. Not that it would do her any good. The crew was aware of the situation and had been on Pablo's payroll for over a decade running guns for him. If anything happened to him, the captain's orders were simple —get the woman to Pablo.

"Please let me go."

He pulled the switchblade from his pocket and thumbed the button. The knife sprung open. "Eat."

"Why are you doing this?" She took a few steps and then stopped.

"Eat." His voice grew loud. He pointed to the tray of food with the knife and then at her. "I'm not telling you again."

The woman sat on the lounge chair, balanced the plastic tray on her lap, and ate.

Cortez took a seat on the bed directly across from her and laid the knife on his right knee. Every now and then she would look at him with such hate in her eyes as if plotting step by step how she was going to kill him in the worst possible way. Then she'd look away and devour her eggs.

When her plate was empty he collected the tray and set it on the desk. He broke the plastic cutlery into small pieces confident they would be useless as a weapon. She may be resourceful but there was no way she could do any damage with the tiny plastic remnants.

He motioned his head toward the bed. "You should sleep for a few hours. It will be daylight soon."

She stood. "I'm getting a drink of water first."

"I will get it for you." Cortez clutched the knife in his hand and turned his body but not his head convinced she'd try something if she had a chance. He got a bottle of water out of the fridge and tossed it to her.

After handcuffing her wrist to the bed, he shut off the lamp and lay on the lounge chair. He could almost hear her thinking out loud in the dark. "If anything happens to me, the captain and crew will take you to Pablo. You might as well get some sleep."

* * *

Blake walked into the coffee shop and found Hal Decker sitting at a booth by the window drinking a cup of coffee.

The man had a mellow yet serious vibe about him that most people would describe as dishonest or possibly dangerous. He was cunning and brilliant. If you didn't know him, at times it was difficult to tell if the guy was a friend or enemy which was exactly what had made him an elite marine and FBI agent. Blake, Hal, and Mike had spent time in the Marines together as part of the multinational peacekeeping force in Beirut in '83. They watched a truck smash into the building where three-hundred Marines were sleeping. Then the driver detonated two-and-a-half-tons of explosives killing two hundred and forty-one American service members. It was a day none of them would ever forget.

As long as Blake could remember, Hal usually kept his blond hair clipped 'high and tight'—marine style—but had let it grow out since the last time Blake had seen him six months ago. Now it came down to the back of his neck at his shoulders and fell a bit over his ears. His new look reminded him of Mike's style—casual undercover cop minus the silver stud earring in one ear.

Hal looked up. "Hey. How you doing?"

Blake managed a weak smile and fidgeted with his keys. "I'm getting by. Could be doing a lot better." He slipped into the booth across from him and set his keys on the table. He watched a teenager giggle and smile at the attractive twenty-something female working behind the counter.

"You want a coffee or something?"

"No, I'm good. Thanks."

Tense silence hung in the air mixed with the sugary scent of freshly baked donuts and coffee.

"My surveillance on the house hasn't produced anything unusual so far. No visitors. After the female occupant, I assume the mother, left this afternoon I went in and planted a few bugs. I'll check the audio when I get back. I have an associate running video while I'm here so we don't miss anything." He took a sip of his drink then set the paper cup down. "I discovered one computer system in a makeshift office and I copied the files and emails." He set a flash drive on the table. "I also found this in the fireplace. It's not much. I'm guessing it's important since it was ripped up and partially burnt. Might lead you to where Whitney could be or where the kidnappers are taking her."

"Kidnapper. We're down to one. Looks like she may have killed the other two. The bodies were dumped on Lenwood under a tree."

Hal grinned. "Good for her."

Yeah. He couldn't agree more. Blake leaned forward and took the clear plastic bag and examined the charred remains of a jagged chunk of paper less than an inch in size. He read the scribbled hand-writing on it. "San Diego Port 7. Shit. They're going by sea. Mike and I discussed the possibility earlier. We just weren't sure if they were heading to San Diego or Los Angeles. Now we pretty much know for sure." He looked at Hal. "But which ship? There are hundreds docked at the port between the personal crafts at the marina, cruise ships, and cargo ships.

I'll contact Customs and Border Protection and Homeland Security. See if we can narrow it down to which ship and confirm its destination. This is great, Hal. I think we finally have something to work with."

"There could be something on here. No idea what's in the files or the emails. There aren't many. Maybe you'll get lucky." He slid the flash drive across the table. "If you need me for anything, and I mean anything—stateside or otherwise—let me know. I'm game. I would really like to have a go at Sanchez."

Blake heard the anger in Hal's voice. He knew the man would take out Sanchez the first chance he got. He'd have to get in line. "I appreciate the offer."

"I should get back. I want to check the video and audio." Hal slid out of the booth and stood. I'll call you when I find out anything else. If you need anything, call. I mean that."

"I will."

Hal stopped and put his hand on Blake's shoulder. "You know there's a good chance she might be already dead."

Blake usually appreciated the man's straightforwardness especially being a former agent, but not this time. Blake quickly dismissed the thought. *She's alive.* "I know."

After Hal left, Blake sat quietly for a few minutes and stared at the burnt piece of paper. He cracked his knuckles and forced himself to concentrate. He was tired and drained but nothing would stop him from finding Whitney. He would bet anything that the '7' on the piece of paper meant seven o'clock—the time the ship was scheduled to leave port. But which ship? And to where?

CHAPTER TEN

The first rays of dawn torched the horizon and gave Blake new hope that he would find Whitney. The morning sunlight glistened off the pavement in the parking lot in front of SecuraCorp. The brightness forced him to close the blinds in his office. He sat at his desk and ran a hand over his tired eyes.

He'd only slept three hours. Not solid sleep. Instead, miserable broken sleep filled with fear. The dream about Whitney preoccupied his thoughts. He had a tough time ignoring the hollow pit of doom ballooning in his stomach. He clenched his jaw. God damn it. He just wanted her home.

He'd already put in a call first thing to Customs and Border Protection and Homeland Security at the San Diego port asking them to fax over copies of all the ships manifests for any vessels that were docked or had set sail, within the last twenty-four hours.

So now he played the waiting game. No telling how long it would be before he had the records and no telling how long it would take to analyze the information. He peered up at the black hands on the wall clock. It was only five-thirty in the morning and he had a growing list requiring his immediate attention, most importantly, finding Whitney and dealing with the blackmailer.

While he waited for Mike, Cally, and McBride to arrive, he rolled up three bundles of newspaper and secured each one with a rubber band then set the rolls inside the black sports bag in preparation for the drop. He zipped up the bag and shoved it beside the desk.

Little did the blackmailer know eyes would be everywhere watching, and Blake was determined to discover who was behind the blackmail attempt. With nothing to lose and a lot to gain—in particular, wreaking havoc in Blake's and Whitney's life—it wouldn't surprise him one bit if Nathan Shaw was somehow involved. Just like the bastard had been involved in his sister Claire's death and so many other innocent lives. He picked up the flash drive Hal had given him and clutched it in the palm of his hand.

Once Vic and his team showed up, Blake would have the guys check the drive and see if there were any other clues as to where Whitney might be. He got up and went to the conference room and made sure there were enough chairs for everyone. While he dragged the last chair across the floor to the table he heard his secretary's excited voice then heard Mike talking.

Michelle stopped in the doorway dressed in a pair of dark gunmetal gray pants, white top, and navy jacket. She pushed her bangs out of her eyes. "Any news about Whitney? I stayed up late watching News3 and didn't hear anymore. I was going to get up early and check again but my alarm didn't go off. I hope she's okay."

Blake noticed Mike standing behind her with the same silly grin on his face as he had yesterday morning, the famous 'you hired her, pal' look.

"There isn't any news. I'll let you know when I hear something. Please hold all my phone calls. I'm waiting for a fax from Customs and Border Protection. I need it right away. It's extremely important."

"Of course." She spun and almost knocked Mike over before rushing down the hallway to her desk in the reception area.

"That woman is way too spunky in the morning." Mike shook his head and handed him a coffee. "Here. Got you an extra-large this morning. Figured you could use."

"Thanks. I didn't sleep much, that's for sure." Blake took the coffee cup and sat at the head of the long wooden table.

Across the room, Vic and his team's 'command center' was cluttered with laptops, electronic equipment, extension cords, notepads, pens, and other electronic gadgets that Blake couldn't even begin to identify.

"I'm interested to see if there is anything on this." Blake set the flash drive on the table and sipped his drink.

Mike stayed standing and leaned against the wall. "How is our friend? I haven't seen him in about eight months."

"The same as always. You know, Hal. He offered—"

"Good morning. McBride said he was on his way." Cally strutted in with dark circles under his eyes, clutching a coffee cup in one hand and a file folder in the other. He passed Blake the file folder. "The IDs on the bodies on Lenwood."

Blake opened the folder and skimmed the contents. "Our guys are Raul and Enzo Arquilla."

"Both have rap sheets a mile long. They've been on the cartel's payroll most of their lives, selling drugs and guns. Basically, doing whatever they're asked to do." Cally pulled up a chair and sat.

"What about the blood in the van?" Mike asked.

"Belongs to Raul. No trace of anyone else's inside or

outside the vehicle."

Blake let out a silent sigh of relief. The news confirmed what he hoped. There was a good chance Whitney was alive. He inhaled a deep breath and released it slowly. "So now we know the name of the last kidnapper, Cortez Guerrero. Any word on how his side-kicks were killed?"

"I checked with the medical examiner. He wasn't too friendly when I woke him up at four-thirty this morning." Cally grinned. "Never liked the man. An arrogant bastard. Anyway, he said from his prelim exam, Raul was stabbed with the nail file found at the scene—a severed carotid artery. He bled out. Enzo had a crushed larynx and trachea due to a hit or kick, but the ME thinks he probably died from blunt force trauma to the back of his head, a possible skull fracture. The autopsies are being done this afternoon and should provide more answers."

"She killed them." Part of Blake was happy Whitney had done what she needed to do to survive so far. He also knew how difficult it would be for her to deal with the aftermath, the guilt of taking a life—multiple lives.

"From what the ME said, yeah, I'd say she did." Cally's voice was filled with pride. "I also spoke with Alberto's ex-girlfriend and his mother after I left Lenwood. Either they don't know anything about Whitney and the kidnapping, or they are covering for Cortez. I'm betting the latter."

Blake figured Cally was probably right but that wasn't helping him get any closer to finding Whitney.

Vic and his team strolled into the room, looking tired and run-down, and settled at the command center table.

"I need you to check this. It might help lead us to Whitney." Blake threw the flash drive to Vic. "See if there is anything in reference to ships. San Diego Port 7. Or travel arrangements of any kind. Anything that might look out of the ordinary."

"We're on it." Vic caught the flash drive in mid-air and handed it to the guy he called the 'Whiz Kid'.

Vic was right. The lanky kid looked like he should be primping for a high school prom not working for the FBI's Cyber Action Team.

"Sorry, I'm late. Had to make a side trip to the park," McBride said.

Blake noticed his unshaven face mirrored the same concern as it did yesterday when they'd learned Whitney had been kidnapped.

McBride shoved a hand into the pocket of his pants and stood in front of the bulletin board facing everyone. "I've got the aerial photo of Freedom Park for this afternoon. The drop is at three thirty." He pinned a color photo to the board and looked at Cally. "You will be here, on the south side by the pool. Mike, you'll be over here next to the public washrooms. I'll stay by the snack bar. Lots of cover but provides an unobstructed view of the drop area. The trash can is located right here." He pointed to the photo and continued. "The moment we see the blackmailer pick up the bag in the can, we move in."

Blake pushed his chair out from the table and stood. "Make sure you're wired-up and ready to go at two forty-five. Then let's nail this bastard."

Whitney hated what she had become. A cold-blooded killer. She tried not to think about the men she had killed, determined to keep the guilt tucked away deep within her. If she thought about Raul and Enzo it would suck the life out of her and zap her energy. Energy she needed right now to save herself.

She wasn't going to allow Cortez to take her to Pablo. She had to get out of this room and find out exactly what she was up against. She'd been awake for hours and the effects of the drug her captor had given were gone.

At least Cortez had removed the handcuff allowing her to move freely around the cabin. While he left to get her something to eat, she'd searched every nook and cranny of the cabin looking for something to use as a weapon but came up empty. He even removed the hangers in the floor-to-ceiling storage closet at the end of the bed. All that was left was a broken flimsy plastic one. The man had done a good job eliminating anything sharp, leaving her with the only weapon available, the one she could rely on—her hands.

After downing breakfast—a delicious vegetable and cheese omelet, coffee, toast, and fresh fruit—in record time, Whitney pushed her empty plate aside on the desk.

She raised her chin and shot her captor a cool stare. "You can't keep me locked up in this room for four days. Please take me on deck so I can get some fresh air. It's not as if I can escape. What am I going to do? Swim to shore?"

Cortez glared at her and didn't say a word. Instead, he folded his arms across his chest as if contemplating the idea.

She prayed he was. It was apparent by the expression on his face, the way his eyes squinted slightly, he didn't trust her.

He shouldn't.

All Whitney needed was one chance to take him out. That time would come soon—at the right moment.

He rubbed the stubble on his chin. His eyes narrowed. "You're correct. You have no place to go except to your death."

His emotionless voice and spooky calm chilled her as much as his words.

She shuddered.

Cortez rose from the chair, reached into the pocket of his black pants, and pulled out a small silver key. He unlocked the handcuff from the bed frame and turned to her. "Put on your shoes."

Relief invaded her veins. She'd convinced him.

"If you cause any problems, I will keep you drugged and secured to the bed until we reach Tumaco. Do you understand?"

No way was Whitney going to allow him to drug her again, otherwise, the next time she woke up she'd be in Colombia. She would have to behave and work on gaining Cortez's trust. Then when he least expected it, she would attack.

"Completely." Whitney slipped on the white canvas running shoes. Her gaze moved to the door and her stomach knotted. She had no clue as to what was awaiting her on the other side.

When Cortez turned to open the door, she spotted her epinephrine autoinjector in his back pocket. At least he'd taken her seriously about her allergy to shellfish.

"Put your hands behind your back."

She glanced at the handcuffs, and then back to him. "Are you kidding? There's no place for me to go."

"This is the only way you are leaving this room." He raised an eyebrow and dangled the metal handcuffs in the air.

Whitney didn't have a choice. If she wanted to investigate some of the ship, she would have to abide by his rules. She turned and put her hands behind her back. Cold steel snapped around her wrists.

Cortez gripped her elbow and spun her to face him. "No games. You walk ahead of me."

She nodded.

He reached around her and opened the door. Then he nudged her in the back. "End of the hall and to the right. The ship has an elevator so we won't have to take thirty flights of stairs to the deck."

Whitney trudged down the well-lit corridor that looked much like a hotel hallway complete with plush carpet and modern art on the walls. It was difficult to believe she was on a cargo ship. Then she noticed a silver and blue plaque on the wall with a name on it—*Trans Venture II*—and realized it was the ship's name.

Inside the elevator, Cortez tightened his grip on her arm. "Aren't the other passengers going to wonder why I'm handcuffed?"

"There aren't any passengers. Only officers and crew. They are fully aware of the situation."

She smiled to herself, grateful for the information he'd provided. Now all she needed to find out was how many crew members were on board. Even if she did, what would she do? She couldn't kill all of them.

Seconds later, the elevator dinged and the door opened.

Bright sunlight and tangy ocean air greeted her. Glistening turquoise water stretched as far as she could see. A larger than life infinity pool. The heat of the sun kissed her face and Whitney sucked in a deep breath of the salty air, grateful to be alive.

For a moment she forgot where she was, that she was a prisoner, and thought about Blake and Angel. There were no words to describe how much she missed them. Her soul ached. So did her heart. *Find a way to get off this ship. Think, Steel.*

"Let's go." Cortez yanked her arm and forced her to walk.

Towering steel containers the size of small houses were stacked four high and filled the deck from bow to stern, looking like a giant maze of metal. The massive cargo creaked and whined against the wind.

As they walked to the other end of the ship, Whitney didn't see anyone. Not a soul, but she did notice the blue, red, and white Panamanian flag blowing in the breeze and remembered a story she had investigated about piracy that international law dictated every merchant must be registered in a country, called a flag state.

When they finally reached the bow, she leaned against the railing and watched the dolphins and flying-fish bound in and out of the water and race through the waves alongside the ship. For the second time, she forgot where she was until she spotted a crew member coming toward them.

The man had the same dark eyes and hair and olive complexion as her captor except his skin was deeply etched from spending years at sea battling the sun and wind.

Cortez took two steps in front of her almost as if trying to block her view and met the man. "What is it?"

"An American ship, fifty miles from here. The captain said you should know."

The man's English was broken and riddled with a thick accent. Whitney looked east and then west and scanned the horizon. All she saw was endless water.

Cortez nodded to the crew member then tugged at her arm and started to drag her across the deck. "Move.

You're going back to the room."

The handcuffs bite into her wrists. "Stop. You're hurting me." She tried to jerk free of his grip and failed.

It was evident by his reaction he was spooked. Whitney wasn't.

The ship could be her ticket home.

She had to figure out how to get to either a radio or satellite phone and call for help.

* * *

After Cally and McBride left, Blake headed down the hallway to his office and waited for Mike to make a phone call. Afterward, they would pay a visit to Cortez Guerrero's wife before meeting the blackmailer. Someone knew something about Whitney and he hoped the man's wife would be helpful. He wasn't counting on it because love trumped everything else even in a life and death situation.

Every space in SecuraCorp reminded Blake of Whitney including his office. He remembered how much she had enjoyed picking out the brown and beige marble floors and light brown paint for the walls. She'd spent endless hours choosing the design and decor. He missed everything about her. Everything.

Blake had barely stepped inside the door when Michelle burst into the room. He swore the woman worked only two speeds. High and overdrive.

"Customs and Border Protection just faxed this over." She plopped a dozen papers on his desk.

"Great." He snatched up the paperwork and flipped through the pages. "Thank you."

"Are you okay? You look pale. Do you want me to get you something to eat?"

As much as he appreciated his secretary's concern all he wanted was five minutes of peace and quiet to gather his thoughts and read the damn fax. He tried retreating again. "I'm fine. Just a bit tired. I'll grab something later."

It did no good. He could tell by the look in her eyes she wasn't going to give up easily.

"You have to eat to keep up your strength. You know, for Whitney."

Her mother-like logic was starting to piss him off. "I'm fully aware I need to eat, Michelle. When I'm hungry I will eat. I don't want to be disturbed for the next few hours unless it's important." Exhaustion weighed him down and his lack of patience had shone through. He needed space to think and he sure as hell couldn't do that with her grilling him about food. Food was the least of his worries. If it was only that simple...

"Fine. If you need anything else, let me know."

"I will." He forced a weak smile and felt bad he'd snapped at her and hurt her feelings. He knew she was only trying to help. "Thanks, Michelle."

After she marched out of the room and disappeared back to the reception area, Blake took a seat behind his desk and began examining the ships' manifests.

"Hey, what's wrong with Michelle? She looks upset."

Blake glanced up at Mike and shook his head. "It's my fault. I lost my patience. I'll deal with her later. Here." He handed him half the stack of papers. "CBP faxed them over."

Mike pulled up a chair and sat down. He kept his elbows on the edge of the desk while he read.

An hour passed, and they finally had a short of list of possible ships.

"Out of five cruise ships, two are heading to Costa Rica,

one to Panama, and two to Colombia. Since it would be difficult to get her aboard without anyone noticing her creating a fuss, I think it's safe to rule them out."

"Agreed." Mike stopped and rubbed his forehead. "I've got three cargo ships. One is heading to Panama, the *Slider Colombia*. Two going to Colombia. The *US Cordoba* and the *TransVenture II*. There's only one personal craft equipped for ocean travel; it's still in dock."

"Can you contact the Harbor Police and have them check out the yacht?"

"I'll get on it."

While Mike made the call, Blake went across the hall to the conference room. He poked his head in the door. "Did you find anything?"

The Whiz Kid looked up from his laptop. "I still have more data to examine yet but I found two emails mentioning the same topic and using basically the same wording. "See you in our homeland. Four days."

Bingo. Colombia. Excitement burst through Blake's veins but was short lived. The kidnapper was taking her to Pablo.

"I checked the destination email address and it's from an account through a free 'use and go' service."

Blake shook his head. "A use and go service? Never heard of it."

"Sort of like your throw-away cell phones. It's a free email service for people who don't have a computer or want to send or receive discreet emails. Kiosks have been popping up in variety stores and independent coffee shops all over the world."

"Sounds like a perfect way for terrorists to communicate." And Cortez and Pablo.

"It is. And difficult to trace." The kid adjusted his

glasses by pushing them higher on his nose.

"The destination email account was probably set up under a fake name. We'll need a court order to get the Internet provider's records and that will take time," Vic said.

"Keep working and let me know the minute you find anything else. What you found so far is gold. Great job."

As Blake walked back to his office, the hellish feeling of doom swelled, and realization set in. Soon Pablo would have Whitney. A man who had slaughtered thousands of men, women, and children…

He took a deep breath and exhaled, determined to force himself to settle down. *Focus on the blackmailer.* He checked his watch. They were still hours away from the drop.

When he entered his office, Mike was eased back in the chair. "Focus on the ships traveling to Colombia. The Whiz Kid found a couple emails on the flash drive Hal gave me. Whitney will be in Colombia in four days. That doesn't give us much time."

"No, it doesn't." Mike straightened in the chair. "The Harbor Police are checking the yacht. They'll contact us if they find anything. The other two ships are the *US Cordoba* and the *TransVenture II*."

"How did Cortez get her on board? Cargo ships only employ twenty to thirty crew members. Someone would have seen something."

"I have no idea, but I'm guessing that Pablo has had this plan in place for a long time. Once we deal with the blackmail issue we need to book a flight to Colombia. We're going to get her back."

"We still have a couple hours to kill before the drop. Let's pay Cortez's wife a—

"This just came." The color had drained from Michelle's face. Her hand shook as he handed him a piece of paper.

Blake grasped the paper and read.

Every sound in the room disappeared. His heartbeat thumped in his ears.

Mike's voice sliced through the silence. "What is it? What's wrong?"

"Pablo Sanchez has a million-dollar bounty on my head."

* * *

Blake white-knuckled the steering wheel of his pickup truck as they drove to The Cocina to talk to Cortez's wife. Fire brewed in his veins. God damnit! How the hell was he going to save Whitney with a price on his head?

There were dozens of guerrilla organizations working in Colombia who funded their operations by kidnapping and using any other means possible to make money. A million dollar windfall would come in handy to help strengthen their illegal activities.

Not only was Blake up against Sanchez, now he had a dozen or more groups—not mentioning individuals—looking to get in on the action determined to be the first to get the million dollars.

"If Pablo faxed the wanted poster, you can bet the bastard sent it to every other crazy nightmare group here in the states as well. Not to mention his cartel buddies in the area."

Mike was right. Nausea rolled in Blake's gut. What the hell was he going to do?

He peered in the side-view mirror then back to the

road. A headache thumped at his temples and made his eyes ache. At this point, he wasn't even safe in the US. Blake had to change his appearance and his identity; it wouldn't be the first time and more than likely not the last he'd have to do this. He remembered bleaching his brown hair to a dirty blond when he worked undercover to nab Nathan Shaw and had used the name Blake Neely.

"We need to find out which ship Whitney is on and get to her before she reaches Colombia. It's our only hope."

"Vic and the guys are still searching the files on the drive and McBride's hitting up his contacts on the street. Chambers thinks you should go underground and let the Bureau take care of things."

Blake laughed. "That's not going to happen. I've never run from anything in my life. I'm not about to start now. Bounty or no bounty. Besides, I'm not putting Whitney's life in Chambers' hands or the Bureau's. If he was in the same situation and it was someone he loved, he wouldn't either."

"I know. That's what I told him."

Ahead, Blake spotted the circular pink and blue sign of The Cocina. He slowed the truck and turned into the parking lot.

"Doesn't appear too busy."

Blake parked and climbed out. Mike met him on the driver's side of the vehicle.

Inside the restaurant, the walls were decorated with wood paneling and there were dark wood tables. The chairs were painted in festive shades of pink and greenish-blue to match the multicolored art work around the square-shaped bar. Blake had to admit the place smelled good, a mixture of beans and beef simmering in fragrant spices and herbs. His stomach growled, reminding him he hadn't eaten.

A woman with shoulder-length black hair, oval brown eyes, and dark olive skin rushed to greet them with a smile.

"Welcome to The Cocina. I'm Isabella."

Blake pulled out his Bureau ID wallet from his back pocket, handed it to her, and waited for her reaction.

She looked at Blake and then to Mike. Lines stretched across her forehead. "Has something happened to Cortez?"

"We need to talk somewhere quiet."

"Of course. In my office." She waved to a male waiter, signaling him to seat the couple who just walked in the door.

Afterward, Blake and Mike followed her down a sterile hallway and entered a small office.

"What is this about?" She handed Blake's ID back to him and appeared even more confused.

"Where is your husband?" Mike asked.

Her eyes widened. "On a buying trip. He takes a plane to Colombia once a month to purchase spices for our most popular meal, fried red snapper, and plantains. Why?"

Yeah, he's on a buying trip alright. Spices? More like cocaine and guns. Blake tried to stay calm only because he needed information. "Has he ever mentioned the *Cordoba* or *TransVenture*?"

"Please tell me what this about." She stuck out her chin. "I'm not answering any more questions until you tell me what's going on." She reached for a cell phone on the desk. "I'm going to call my sons."

Mike grabbed her hand to stop her from using the phone. He shook his head. "Don't."

Nerves stretched to the breaking point. "Damn it. Just answer the question. Have you or not?" Blake's voice was hard and he knew it. He didn't care. He had no more time for games. "Look, lady. The woman I love was kidnapped this morning. Has your husband ever mentioned either of those names? Think."

She looked at Blake with blank eyes. She was about to check out on him and he needed to stop that from happening and now.

"Raul and Enzo Arquilla are dead. Your husband took my fiancée."

Isabella's mouth gaped open, clearly in disbelief. A few seconds passed before she spoke again.

"I heard Cortez talk to Raul on the phone once, something about the *TransVenture*. But I don't even know what it is."

"It's a ship, lady. A cargo ship. Your husband is taking my fiancée to Colombia, to Pablo Sanchez, where she will probably die."

Saying the words made it all too real. Sour bile crept up his throat and Blake fought to force it down. He inhaled a deep silent breath and then exhaled.

The woman's hand went to her mouth and she gasped. "My God. The reporter on the news yesterday morning."

"Yes."

She shook her head and tears filled her eyes. "I can't believe Cortez is involved. I just can't. He's not a horrible man."

"Believe me, he is." *And he's involved in a lot more.* He didn't have the heart to tell her the details. Learning that your husband is a kidnapper was probably more than enough for one day.

Mike removed the phone from her hand and set it on

the desk. "Is there anything else you might have over-heard? It's important."

"Not that I can think of. All I know is my husband is due back in seven days. Just like he always does when he goes on his trips to Colombia. He goes for a week."

Blake was confident that Isabella didn't know any-thing else. "Thanks." He glanced at Mike and then nodded toward the door.

"What's going to happen to Cortez?"

Blake turned and saw it. The sadness in her eyes. "I don't know."

In the parking lot, he paced in front of the truck while Mike called Chambers.

Minutes later Mike finished the call. "Chambers is working on getting the location of the *TransVenture*. He's got a helicopter on standby."

"Good. Once this blackmail gig is done, we're out of here." He patted Mike on the back. "We're going to bring Whitney home."

CHAPTER ELEVEN

Pablo sat across from Alejandro on the terrace high in the mountains above the Bogotá River. The temperature hovered around seventy degrees, the sun hot against the back of Pablo's neck. Leaves from one of the soaring palm trees swayed in the breeze surrounding the pool.

"The wanted poster was faxed to Blake Barnett," Alejandro said.

"And to the others?"

"Yes. Our network in the United States has been notified and our underground connections as well."

Pablo smiled. He could visualize the former FBI agent's face when he learned about the bounty. "Good work, Hermano. Things are moving according to plan."

"They are. This latest action will ensure your protection and also make sure he is brought directly to us. He will not have the chance to try to kill you. Nor will he have the chance to rescue his woman."

Pablo took a sip of his coffee then set the cup on the glass table. He did have a knack for bribing people to play for the right team. A million dollar bounty spoke loudly.

So did threats.

He was feared by everyone. He'd earned that right. The law of the land. His land and his law. Do as you're told, or you and your loved ones will pay the price. His law had been drilled into the minds of Colombians for years and by others for decades before him. Pablo was just doing his job, what was expected of him. He had to admit at times killing sometimes aroused him. Not the act itself, but the power and control he had over a person he was about to kill—to watch them beg with their eyes...

Pablo couldn't wait to get his hands on Blake Barnett and Whitney Steel. It wouldn't be much longer.

He smiled then took a bite of the chocolate croccantino crepe and downed it with a mouthful of coffee.

Alejandro finished his heaping bowl of Ajiaco, made with chicken, corn, and potatoes that Pablo's cook had specifically prepared for him, then set his spoon down. He leaned back in the chair and dabbed the sweat from his brow with his cloth napkin.

Pablo noticed Alejandro was much quieter than usual. The man had a certain sorrow in his eyes over the deaths of Raul and Enzo. Pablo's jaw tightened. He didn't like seeing his friend upset. The man was like a father to him. Whitney Steel would pay very much like Blake Barnett.

He lit a cigar and relaxed back in the chair, watching the two young blondes he'd paid a thousand dollars each for doing laps in the pool wearing skimpy bikinis. He would enjoy their company later and then tell them they would be drug mules for the cartel. They would thank him for such a privilege, for rescuing them from a lifetime of working in sweat shops like their fat mothers.

Eduardo walked toward him, his sidearm glistening in the sunlight. "This just arrived."

Pablo sat up and took the paper from his guard and unfolded it. The message was from the captain of the *Trans-Venture II*. He read it.

"El americano transporta cincuenta millas de nosotros. Aconsejar."

Alejandro turned and looked him. "An American ship so close could mean trouble in more ways than one."

His associate was correct. Pablo crumpled the paper in his hand and threw it toward the pool. His muscles tensed.

Nothing could go wrong.

Not now.

Not when he had waited years for revenge.

❋ ❋ ❋

After leaving The Cocina and grabbing a quick lunch of ham and cheese submarine sandwiches, Blake and Mike returned to SecuraCorp. While Mike packed up everything they would need for the drop, Blake made a quick phone call to his father.

Blake wasn't taking any chances. With a bounty on his head, he needed to make sure everyone around him remained safe, and that included his secretary.

"Michelle arrived ten minutes ago. The young lady is not happy about going into hiding," his father said.

"It's for her own good." The safe house was the best place for her. She fought Blake every step of the way but eventually, he won.

"Are you going to tell me exactly what's going on, son? Michelle won't tell me a thing. Something has changed. I know it."

Blake paced in front of the window of his office. His father wasn't stupid. He was going to have to bullshit his way through this one. "Just believe me when I say everything is okay. I just don't like taking chances when Nathan Shaw and Pablo Sanchez are involved." He quickly changed the subject, determined to stop him asking more questions. "How are Angel and mom?"

"Your mother's fine. A bit tired and worried like usual. That sweet little girl is keeping her busy. Angel is doing well except she misses you and Whitney. Right now, she's painting a picture for both of you. She's quite the artist for her age." He cleared his throat. "Any more news on Whitney?"

The thought of Angel missing him tugged at Blake's heartstrings. In a few more days things would be back to normal. "We know she's on a ship heading to Colombia. The Bureau is working on getting the ship's exact location. Then we're going to get her."

"That's good news. Be careful, Blake. Colombia is not a safe place."

Blake heard Angel's infectious giggle in the background and then heard his mother laughing. "It is. Anyway, I need to go. I'll call you as soon as I have some more news. And Dad? If you get the feeling something isn't right or if anything happens, get everyone to the panic room. Help will arrive immediately."

"I will. Don't worry. Nothing is going to happen on my watch, son. Talk to you soon."

Blake ended the call and smiled at his father's typical marine type response. But Blake was worried. With a price on his head, someone could discover a way to get to him just like Pablo was using Whitney to get to him. He drew a deep breath and slipped on his Kevlar vest and secured the Velcro tabs.

This was the first time he'd worn a bulletproof vest since being shot by Nathan Shaw while he and Whitney rescued Angel from Shaw's cloning lab at ShawBioGen. Blake tried not to think about that night and how he almost died. He pulled on a short-sleeved black shirt over top of the vest and buttoned it.

Mike strutted into the office. "Cally and McBride are ready to roll." He handed Blake an earpiece and mic.

"Good." Blake slipped on a ball cap and attached the mic to the collar of his shirt. He stuck the earpiece in his ear and adjusted it. "Cally, McBride. Can you hear me?"

"Check."

"Yup," McBride said.

Mike nodded.

Blake glanced at his watch. Two thirty-five. They had to leave within the next ten or fifteen minutes to allow for enough time to get to the park. He bent and picked up the black sports bag from the floor filled with rolled up newspapers.

"Showtime."

❋ ❋ ❋

Thirty minutes later, Blake wheeled the pickup truck off North Mojave Road and into the parking lot at Freedom Park.

The lot was filled with about two dozen vehicles made up mostly of mini-vans. Mike sat in the passenger seat with his head tilted back on the headrest.

Blake couldn't wait to learn the identity of blackmailer and more importantly exactly who was pulling the strings. In the rear-view mirror, he watched Cally and McBride pull up in the silver SUV and park beside them. He shifted in the seat. The weight of the bulletproof vest made his shoulder and chest ache where Nathan had shot him.

Mike unfolded the map of the park and spread it out across his knees. "Cally. South side of the pool. McBride will be at the snack bar. I'll be by the public restrooms."

"Got it," McBride and Cally said in unison. They climbed out of the SUV and Cally gave Blake a thumbs-up as they walked by.

Mike folded the map and tucked it back in the glove box then exited the vehicle.

Blake peered at the clock on the dash. Sixteen minutes after three. He pulled out his 9 mm Glock from under the seat and hopped out of the truck. After stuffing the gun into the waistband of his jeans, he grabbed the sports bag out of the trunk and drew a long breath. "I don't like that this is going down around a bunch of kids."

"That's probably why the guy chose the pool area. Protection for himself. We'll keep our eyes peeled." Mike patted him on the shoulder. "Let's get this asshole."

He nodded and waited for Mike to get at least halfway to the restroom area before making his move. Strolling along the winding sidewalks, Blake scanned the tree line and then around the pool searching for anything appearing out of place. He never liked jumping in blindly. This was one of those times. They could easily be walking into a trap.

Blake slowed his pace a few yards from the trashcan and clutched the handles of the sports bag.

"I'm in place," Cally said. "Nothing out of the ordinary."

"Me too," McBride added.

"I have a woman with two kids gawking at me like I'm a pedophile hanging out at the restrooms. Going to take a hike so she doesn't get suspicious and call the locals."

Blake kept his head lowered and made his way to the trash can. "Roger that." When he was confident no one was watching, he dropped the bag in the can then walked away.

Children splashed about in the pool, voices filled with laughter and excitement. If they only knew what was going on behind the scenes.

Blake waited for what seemed like forever. He checked his watch. Three thirty-nine. The blackmailer was late. "See anyone yet? I'm at the snack bar. Just ordered a drink."

"Nothing," McBride said.

Cally cleared his throat. "Nope."

"Wait," Mike said. "Male. Red hat. Black T-shirt and black jeans,"

Blake turned his head and watched.

The man reached into the trashcan and pulled out the sports bag. He looked left then right before he spun and walked briskly away.

"Go!" Blake dropped his drink and ran through the long line of parents waiting at the snack bar and almost knocked a young woman off her feet.

Mike and Cally raced ahead of him while Blake eyed McBride circling around the pool trying to cut the man off.

The man disappeared behind a covered picnic area and out of sight.

McBride took one side and stood guard. Mike stayed low and sprinted to the other side and waited. Blake and Cally stopped in the middle of a dozen tables partially filled with families. "Get them out of here, Cally."

As Cally herded the families far enough from the scene, Blake bent at the waist with both hands on his knees gasping to catch his breath. "The bastard has nowhere to go."

"I'm going in." Mike pulled his gun from the back of his

jeans and flattened his body against the metal structure. He inched his way to the end and peeked around the corner. "He's leaning against the back wall."

"Roger." McBride already had his gun drawn and crept his way alongside the wall until he reached the end. "Ready?"

The wind kicked up and sent an updraft of dust flying in the air. Blake's earpiece crackled. "Now!"

Both McBride and Mike disappeared from Blake's view and he heard them yelling at the man.

Seconds later, McBride strutted around the corner with a grin on his face and his hand groped around the back of the man's neck. Mike walked beside them, his weapon pointed at the ground and in his other hand was the black sports bag.

"Get your hands off of me." The man wiggled trying to get out of McBride's grasp.

McBride swatted the kid in the back of the head and sent his ball cap flying.

Blake went to meet them.

The man appeared to be in his twenties with black hair clipped short and a well-trimmed beard. He was tall and wiry like an overgrown weed.

"Let's get him to the truck," Blake said.

"You can't just kidnap me."

"We sure can. Hell, we just did." McBride laughed and flashed the kid his Bureau ID.

The kid rolled his eyes and shook his head.

When Blake turned, a large crowd had gathered— mainly mothers with kids. The women appeared worried while children stared with wide eyes, transfixed on what had just gone down.

"Everything is fine. Show's over folks. We got the bad

guy."

As they walked back to the vehicles, Blake spotted a camera man and a female reporter with long blonde hair running toward them. This was the last thing he needed. "Damn it!"

Mike slipped his gun behind his back. "Shit. Someone at the park must have called them."

Or a carefully orchestrated move by whoever was behind the blackmail attempt. "Get him in the SUV." Blake removed his earpiece and mic and shoved them in the pocket of his jeans. As the reporter got closer, bile rose in his throat and turned his mouth bitter. He didn't like dealing with reporters, especially the young ones. Too in your face and ambitious.

"Mr. Barnett. Any news about your fiancée?"

"No comment." He picked up his pace and tried to dodge her but she was glued to his hip jogging beside him in high heels.

"Does that man have something to do with her kidnapping?"

He remained silent and kept walking.

"Are you aware Pablo Sanchez has a bounty on your head? Is he back in the US?"

Blake stopped dead in his tracks. His jaw tightened. How did she know? He stared at the woman, determined to find out. "Shut off the camera."

The woman nodded to the camera guy. "Cut it."

The red light on the camera turned off.

Blake glared at the reporter. "Who told you about the bounty?"

"It came through the news room by fax a few hours ago. Then we got a phone tip twenty minutes ago that you were here in the park."

Tip my ass. He sidestepped the reporter and could tell by the pinched expression on her face she knew he was going to dodge her.

"Hey, wait. Can you tell me something?"

Blake shook his head and trudged past her and headed to the truck. Someone was playing games and he was bloody-well going to find out who.

Back at SecuraCorp, Blake slammed his office door closed and narrowed his eyes at the kid sitting in the chair. "Okay, asshole. You've got exactly five seconds to tell me who paid you to hack into our network and steal our confidential files."

The guy looked down at his hands and then up at Blake. He shrugged. "I don't know what you're talking about."

Blake picked up the aged brown wallet on his desk and searched the contents. He pulled out a driver's license and held it up. "Jake Michael Robson, you're going to do some pretty serious federal time for stealing FBI documents. Minimum fifteen years. Four."

His eyes widened and his mouth dropped open. "Fifteen years?"

"Naw. Maybe twenty. You'll be what—forty-four when you get out? Three."

"Okay. Okay." The kid shook his head. "A friend of mine is doing time for robbery. A couple months ago I visited him. He said he knew a guy inside who needed a special job done using my particular skill set. Paid five thousand dollars cash. He said all I needed to do was hack into a computer and threaten to post some personal stuff. That's it."

"Which prison is your 'friend' doing time in?" Blake had a feeling he already knew.

"Ely State."

Blake balled his fists. Ely State Prison. Nathan Shaw's home until he was supposed to be transferred to death row at Nevada State Prison in Carson City.

"So you weren't going to send the files to the newspapers or post them online?"

The kid scratched the side of his head. "Nope. That wasn't what I was paid for. After reading some of the files, no way was I releasing anything. Not my style. I was paid to hack and threaten. Nothing more."

"Well aren't you just Mr. Noble." Blake was relieved to know the confidential information from their network computer wasn't going anywhere and the agents involved would be safe. "Did anyone mention why they wanted the job done?"

"Something about keeping you busy. Have no idea why."

Blake did. Every muscle in his body tightened. He wanted to throttle the kid and it took all his willpower not to.

They wanted to keep Blake distracted because the time wasted working on figuring out who was behind the blackmail attempt and going to the 'so called' drop gave Cortez time to get Whitney out of the country undetected because they knew Blake would take the time protect the agents involved. Now Whitney and her kidnapper had a good day's head start.

The plan had worked.

Whitney's wrists burned. She rubbed the raw and

bruised skin where the handcuffs dug into her skin from Cortez dragging along the deck. He'd dumped her back in the cabin then disappeared in a hurry, concerned about the news of a ship in the area.

She paced the room and swallowed the hard lump in her throat. If she tried to get to a radio or satellite phone and call for help and didn't succeed, her captor would drug her and she'd wake up in Colombia, her chance of getting help gone. A nip of fear sent her heart hammering.

What did she have to lose? If she didn't try, Cortez would take her to Pablo anyway. If she tried and failed, same outcome.

At the moment, her life had value to her captor. No one dare kill her, at least not until she got to Colombia, and she was betting Pablo was looking forward to that honor. From what Cortez had said, everyone on the ship had their orders—to get her to Pablo no matter what.

Whitney opened the mini fridge, took out a bottle of water, and gulped down half the bottle.

I have no choice. Blake would expect nothing less from her, to try to save herself any way possible.

She grabbed her purse from the table and quickly dug through it until she found an elastic band then put her hair in a high ponytail.

Cortez would be back in fifteen to twenty minutes. He never left her alone for long periods of time. She had to hurry.

Whitney glanced around the cabin. Since everything sharp had been removed, she didn't have much to choose from but had to come up with something to use. The table lamp.

She hurried to the desk and yanked the electrical cord from the outlet then lifted the lamp and felt the heavy brass base in her hand, satisfied it would work. If she succeeded should she hike up the thirty flights of stairs or take the elevator to the deck? Both carried their risks and challenges especially since she had no idea how many crew members were on board. She would have to decide once she got out of the room. She snatched up her shoulder bag at the end of the bed and looped the handles over her head, letting the purse rest on her hip.

After taking off the cream-colored cloth shade and unscrewing the light bulb, she wound the cord tightly around the base. Whitney inhaled a deep breath and let it out. Anticipation made her knees feel as if they would buckle under her. She didn't like the thought of possibly having to kill again.

What choice did she have?

Fisting the base of the lamp with both hands as if she was about to bat a home run, Whitney stood behind the door and waited for her captor to return.

CHAPTER TWELVE

On the ship's sterile bridge, the white tiled floors glistened with wax in the sunlight. Cortez watched Captain Dabon, a short Panamanian with olive skin and a brown bushy mustache, blot his sweaty forehead with the sleeve of his white shirt.

Cortez had known the captain for more than ten years and trusted him completely. If Dabon was sweating while the air conditioning on the bridge blasted cool air, the man was worried and that concerned Cortez even more. "What type of ship is it?"

Dabon peered through a large set of binoculars while the helmsman and pilot kept their eyes straight ahead. "Looks like American military. They're gaining speed. It could be problematic."

Another ship, particularly an American one, had Cortez's nerves buzzing. Did they know the woman was aboard? The last thing he needed was a wrinkle in the plan. He had to get the woman to Pablo. He couldn't get caught.

For over twenty-five years, Pablo had used the *Trans-Venture* and two other cargo ships to deliver large caches of guns and cocaine to the United States. Not once had any of the ships been stopped or searched thanks to his well-paid and occasionally threatened network of thousands in the US and in Colombia. Everything always ran smoothly. If it didn't, Pablo would ensure it did one way or another, including with blood.

The helmsman looked down at the radar screen and then turned to Cortez. "They are about twenty miles to the southwest."

He didn't like the ship so close. And he didn't like surprises. Especially ones that could land him in jail. Maybe he was being paranoid. "Perhaps the ship is doing some type of practice manoeuvres? I think I'll go and secure the woman to be safe."

Dabon snapped his fingers and made a hand signal to the ship's helmsman. The man nodded and took his place while the captain walked with Cortez to the bridge door. "We must be cautious with your priceless cargo. I will keep you informed of any changes as to the military ship."

✽ ✽ ✽

Whitney shifted from foot to foot, her hands sore from gripping the lamp's base. It had been thirty minutes and she wondered if Cortez was ever going to return. She steeled her nerves for what was about to happen. She had to do this.

Hurt or be hurt. Live or die.

Her captor had given her no choice.

She heard the key click in the lock.

She held her breath, bent her knees slightly, and dug the heels of her bare feet into the carpet for traction.

The door flew open.

Cortez walked inside and stopped as if he sensed something was wrong.

She extended her arms, exhaled, then swung the

lamp.

The metal base smacked the back of his skull with a loud crack like lightning hitting a tree. The sound almost made Whitney sick to her stomach.

The force of the hit slammed Cortez forward to his knees. His body jerked. He rocked back and forth, his arms flailing.

She prayed he'd fall over and pass out. He didn't.

"You bitch!" He jumped to his feet and barreled toward her, his body low like a bull ready to gore her.

Whitney pivoted on her left foot, stretched out her right leg high, and smashed him in the mouth with her heel thrusting him off balance.

Two teeth flew through across the room and landed on the desk. A fine mist of red sprayed against the leg of her jogging pants.

Cortez staggered, his body shaking. He stared at her with narrow dark eyes as he wiped the blood from his mouth with the back of his hand.

She couldn't allow him to get the upper hand. She ran at him and shoved the palm of her hand into the bridge of his nose. He hurtled backwards flipping over the back of the sofa and onto the floor with a thud.

His jaw gaped open. Blood streamed from his nose and ran down his T-shirt. Cortez shook his head. Droplets of blood showered the coffee table. He jumped to his feet. "You're a dead woman." He reached into the pocket of his pants for his switchblade.

She leapt over the couch, and in a tornado of movement, delivered a roundhouse kick to the side of her captor's head. His jaw cracked. He spun a half-circle and dropped to the floor where he lay motionless on his side.

Whitney's legs buckled and she crumpled to the carpet.

She sat there for a couple seconds, her body trembling, and stared at Cortez. Blood continued to pour from his nose and mouth, carving a red river down his chin. On the right side of his face, red and purple bruises had formed and mingled with smeared blood.

She crawled across the floor and rolled him onto his back. Her hands shook as she lowered her head to his chest.

God, he was still breathing. Her heart sank. Part of her wanted him to die so she wouldn't have to kill him.

Whitney searched each pocket in Cortez's jeans and pulled out the switchblade and the handcuffs along with the key. In his back pocket, she snatched her autoinjector and tossed the medicine into her shoulder bag.

She dragged his body six feet to the bed and slipped one of the handcuffs around his wrist, clicked it closed, and then secured the other one to the metal bed frame.

Afterward, she ran into the bathroom and scrubbed the blood from her hands and face, barely able to look at herself in the mirror for what she had done and for what she had also done to Raul and Enzo.

She looked down at the dark blood splattered on the bottom of her jogging pants. The stains could be a dead giveaway that something was wrong if she was stopped on the way to the deck. Whitney rushed back into the main living area and grabbed the other pair of pants Cortez had given her.

After shoving her feet into the canvas shoes, she clutched the knife handle in her hand and inhaled a long steady breath and let it out. She needed a gun, but the switchblade would have to do.

Live or die.

Whitney placed her hand on the door knob and turned it slowly. The door clicked and then opened. She peeked down the stretch of hallway and didn't see anyone. Half walking, half running, she stopped at the elevator and slid the switchblade into the pocket of the sweatshirt. The best she could do was to pretend Cortez had allowed her to visit the deck. But convincing anyone along the way might not be as easy as it sounded.

As the elevator door spread open to the ship's deck, Whitney said a silent prayer. She needed to find a radio or satellite phone.

She stepped onto the deck. Sunshine had been replaced with dark, threatening clouds. Wind whistled and creaked between the cargo containers sounding like metal cables twisting ready to snap. The gale force wind almost knocked her off her feet, pushing at the back of her legs as she crept behind the stairs leading to the bridge.

It was now or never. No turning back.

The wind whipped through her hair. Her ponytail slapped against the side of her face. Whitney shoved her nerves and hair aside and pulled Cortez's switchblade from her pocket. Her thumb barely touched the button and the knife sprung open. She held the weapon down at her side and began climbing the first set of steel stairs. Every few seconds she glanced over her shoulder, expecting to see a crew member behind her but it never happened.

Gripping the railing with one hand, she stopped on the first landing. Massive waves crashed against the side of the ship and then the sea disintegrated into churning chaotic swells.

Whitney continued up the stairs, her instincts on high

alert. She'd passed the third landing and thought she heard footsteps behind her. Goosebumps erupted over her skin and sent a chill through her body. She spun.

No one. Only the wind so she thought.

Voices. The smell of cigarette smoke.

She looked directly above her two floors up on the landing. Two crew members dressed in white shirts and black pants.

Whitney stepped backwards until she was safely hidden under the landing, out of their view. Crouching, she waited and listened to them speak in Spanish but couldn't understand what they were saying. A few minutes later, she felt the vibration of their heavy footsteps head upwards, obviously to the bridge.

Waves splashed over the side of the ship and drenched the deck below with water and foam.

There had to be more than two crew members on a ship this size. Where was everyone else? The person who had cooked her meals? Where was the man who told Cortez about the American ship? Was he on the bridge with the captain? A shiver tingled up the back of her neck. Whitney wished she knew what she was about to walk into. Five crew members? Twenty? She had no clue.

She scampered up two more floors, stopped, and looked up. The last set of white stairs led to the bridge. The weather was getting worse. Waves pounded the side of the ship. Rain whipped at her face. A gust of wind tugged at her legs and made it difficult to walk. She fought against it and finally made it to the last landing.

Whitney ducked and edged past the windowed bridge until she was hiding in the corner right outside the door. Raising slowly and just enough to peek in the window, she spotted four men. Two wearing white shirts. Two dressed all in black.

If she could convince them that her captor had fallen, she might be able to clear the bridge of one or two of the men, bettering her odds. Whitney would need to put on the performance of a lifetime.

She closed the switchblade and tucked the knife back in her pocket.

This had better work.

After silently counting to three she swung open the door and barged inside.

Four men stared at her with wide eyes, surprised by her abrupt and unexpected entrance.

A short man with brown hair and a thick mustache who appeared to be the captain took two steps then stopped. "What are you doing up here?"

Another officer with a white shirt grasped her forearm. He smelled like cigarette smoke and cheap aftershave. He must have been one of the men she'd seen on the landing.

"It's Cortez. He fell down the stairs. He's hurt badly." She looked the captain straight in the eye and fought to keep her knees from shaking. "He needs help now." *Please believe me.*

The captain turned to the two men dressed in black on either side of him and said, "Get the doctor and check on Cortez."

While the men scurried out the door, Whitney spotted the satellite phone at the other end of the bridge next to a bank of equipment with dozens of dials and buttons. She didn't have much time. It wouldn't be long before the men learned the truth about Cortez.

Whitney jerked her arm free then landed a double palm heel blow to the officer's ears, catching the man off guard.

He doubled over clutching his head.

She grabbed both his shoulders, raised her knee and rammed it up and into the man's nose, sending him flying backwards into a row of control panels on the wall.

His body hit with an echoing tinny thud. Blood streamed from his broken nose. He moaned then slowly slid down the wall into a motionless heap.

The captain tried to snag her arm.

She spun out of his way and snatched the switchblade out of her pocket. The blade sprang open. "Don't move an inch or you will end up like him."

He looked down at his officer out cold on the floor then back to her. He didn't move a muscle.

Whitney held her ground. Keeping the knife pointed at him, she stepped backwards until she reached the satellite phone. The receiver was much heavier and bulkier than she imagined.

Just one call.

"You will not get away with this." The captain's eyes narrowed, his voice hard and threatening.

The truth hit with a belly punch of realization. He was right.

She wouldn't get away with it. If anything, Whitney would pay dearly in a matter of minutes—perhaps even with her own life.

Before leaving Jake the blackmailer in the conference room with Vic and his team, Blake left orders to shoot the kid if he tried anything funny. As far as Nathan was concerned, there wasn't much Blake could do. Even with proof the bastard had orchestrated the blackmail attempt, it wouldn't change the outcome. Nathan Shaw would still be executed. Final justice.

Now with a bounty on his head, Blake was forced to change his looks. He didn't have a choice. He'd spent the past two hours bleaching his hair blond and applying a fake lotion tan. He peered in the bathroom mirror at his newly colored locks. Christ, he looked like a wannabe surfer dude with spiky hair who'd been hanging at the beach for weeks. He put on the silver wire-framed glasses to complete his new look.

Minutes later he strolled into his office. "Well?"

Mike burst out laughing. "Hey, dude. Surf's up."

Blake smacked him in the arm as he walked by. "Smartass. At least it'll be difficult to recognize me compared to Pablo's wanted poster."

"Hell, I almost didn't recognize you," McBride said with a huge grin on his face.

"We have another problem." Mike scratched his head. "The media's camped out front. The parking lot's full."

That was a problem Blake didn't need. "Shit." He could guarantee the female reporter at Freedom Park earlier was probably leading the parade pack, itching to get a story.

"There is good news though. Hal said he'd meet us at the airfield."

Blake was happy Hal had offered to help. Three former Marines. Nothing but the best to get Whitney off that ship.

He looked at McBride leaning back in the chair. "You sure you and Cally can handle things here?"

"No problem. Chambers added some extra security in case anyone comes snooping around thinking they can collect on that reward. There's a sharp-shooter on the roof across the street and a dozen locals within a half block."

Blake had to admit he was floored by his old boss' generosity, considering how many times he and Chambers had butted heads over the years. Blake remembered the last run-in he'd had with the man. Blake had run a background check on his former SAC after he became suspicious that Chambers may be playing for the wrong team—Nathan Shaw and Pablo Sanchez's side. At the time, Blake wasn't going to put Angel's life in danger after Sanchez had kidnapped her and he made that damn clear.

Mike shook his head. "Oh, man, Chambers is irate. He found out about the financial check."

"I'll deal with him later." Blake rubbed his chest.

"Umm...too late." Mike pointed over his shoulder. "He's stalking this way."

Blake turned.

In the light, the man's face was red. His eyes were narrowed. Both arms were at his side, his hands clenched into tight fists.

"Shit," Mike said.

"Shit is right." Blake didn't have time for this.

Chambers stopped and faced him. He loosened his tie. "How dare you run a financial check on me. What the fuck do you think you're doing? Last I checked, you and Jacobs resigned last week. You're off this case. I'm sending another agent to meet Sanchez."

Not a chance in hell.

Blake had had enough. He was tired and sore. "Fuck you. You saw the DVD. You know Sanchez's terms." He gritted his teeth. "I might have had to put up with your bullshit for thirteen years, but you are not putting that little girl's life in jeopardy. Now, get the hell out of my way."

He pushed Chambers to one side.

The shrill sound of his cell phone ringing gave Blake a jerk. He snatched the phone from his desk and answered the call. "Barnett."

"Oh, God. It's so good to hear your voice. I miss you so much."

She was alive. "Whitney." Hearing her voice meant everything. "Honey, are you okay? Did they hurt you?"

"No, I'm okay. But I can't talk long. They'll be back soon. I'm on a cargo ship. The *TransVenture*. Blake, someone named Cortez is taking me to Pablo Sanchez."

He heard her voice tremble, the fear in each word. If only he could reach through the phone and save her. "I know. We're coming to get you. Me, Mike, and Hal. The chopper's ready. We'll be there soon. I promise."

"If something happens to me—know that I love you with all my heart, body, and soul. Hug and kiss Angel for me. I know you'll give her a wonderful life. You're going to be an amazing father."

I love you with all my heart, body, and soul. Those were exact words Blake had said to her the day he had proposed, the same day he also told her she was safe, that Pablo wasn't a threat.

"No. Stop talking like that. We're going to get married and raise Angel together. Honey, do you hear me? Together."

A long pause filled with silence.

Mike and McBride huddled around him. Worry electrified the air.

"Whitney? Are you still there? Whitney!"

"Yes. Together. I have to go. They're coming up the stairs. Oh, God..."

"Fight, baby. Fight. I'm on my way. I love you."

Dead silence.

It was if his whole life had been sucked out from under him—the thought of losing her weighed heavy in his soul, the anguish unbearable. *I should have protected you.*

"God damn it!" He picked up his empty coffee cup and heaved it across the room. The cup bounced off the bookcase and shattered into pieces onto the floor.

He looked at Mike. "We have to go now. I don't know how much longer she has." Blake grabbed his Kevlar vest from the back of his desk chair. "We need to save Whitney."

❋ ❋ ❋

As evening blanketed Las Vegas, Blake, Mike, and Hal ran to the Bell UH-1H helicopter at Henderson Executive Airport. The downdraft of the main rotor roared a blast of typhoon-force air around them.

Blake protected his eyes from the dust and debris and hopped into the front seat of the helicopter while Mike and Hal took a seat on the four-man bench behind him. Blake slid the door closed.

Inside the cabin, the cockpit lights reflected a kaleidoscope of greens and blues on the windshield. Blake put on his headset then locked his seatbelt. He looked at the male pilot. "How long before we're in the area of the ship?"

"About an hour." The pilot started pushing buttons, flipping switches, and levers. "Be warned. There's a storm brewing. Might be a rough ride."

Blake couldn't care less how rough the ride was as long as he was able to bring Whitney home. He glanced out the side window at the airport as the helicopter vibrated slightly. The chopper's landing skids bounced then lifted off the tarmac. The ground quickly shrunk below them.

A painful hollowness filled his chest and his heart lurched at the thought of Whitney fighting for her life. He prayed she was still alive. She had to be. He couldn't imagine Cortez killing her. Whitney was Pablo's ticket to Blake. Pablo wanted him.

As the helicopter flew over the city, Las Vegas looked like an oversized Christmas display lit to the hilt, the colorful lights twinkled against the cloudy sky. While Hal and Mike chatted, Blake leaned his head against the headrest. His mind raced, and reality sucker punched him in the gut. He felt like he was in a movie and someone kept hitting the rewind button. Last time it was Nathan Shaw trying to kill him and Whitney. This time it was Pablo. Yet all the same players were involved. He clenched his fists. At least Shaw would eventually be executed. Too bad it wasn't tomorrow. And Blake would make damn sure Pablo Sanchez would never have the chance to threaten them again.

Thirty minutes later the pilot adjusted his headset. "We're about to fly into some nasty stuff."

Blake straightened in the seat and peered through the windshield. Heavy rain whipped against the glass. Wind tugged at the side of the helicopter. "How much longer?"

The pilot reached a control panel and flipped a few more switches. "Twenty."

"The weather's going to make it difficult to get aboard," Hal said.

"It's going to be tough," Mike said. "Not something we haven't dealt with before though."

Mike was correct. The three men had seen their share of extreme weather while in the Marines, from wind storms to sand storms to tropical storms.

The spotlight on the nose of the aircraft revealed the rolling swell of the ocean. Waves rose, then dropped. It wasn't going to be easy to rappel to the deck of the ship, especially with the wind. But it was doable.

No chance in hell was Blake going to abort the mission.

One way or another he was going to get on that ship.

Whitney was coming home.

CHAPTER THIRTEEN

In the brightly lit infirmary, one of the men dressed in all black from the bridge stood guard with a gun pointed at her. Whitney sat handcuffed to a chair and watched the ship's doctor stitch up the wide laceration on the back of her captor's head where she'd struck him with the lamp.

She had failed.

He was alive.

She'd also failed on the bridge.

Three men with guns against one.

Whitney had been outnumbered. At least Blake knew where she was. She prayed he'd be here soon.

When the doctor was done, Cortez lifted his head and stared at her. The skin under his eyes was black and blue, his nose swollen and crooked with gauze sticking out of both nostrils.

"Your jaw isn't broken. You're lucky, my friend. It's going to be sore for some time." The doctor opened a bottle of pills and handed Cortez two of them. "They should help with the pain and headache from the broken nose."

Whitney noticed the man didn't have an accent like the others she'd encountered on the ship.

Cortez popped the pills in his mouth and swallowed them without water. He glared at her, his eyes narrow slits. "I should throw you overboard for what you have done."

She jutted out her chin and stared back at him, determined not to back down knowing he had to keep her alive.

The doctor pulled out a hypodermic needle and a clear vial of liquid from a large metal chest filled with medical supplies. "You sure about this?"

Cortez nodded. "She must be put out again. It's for her own good as well as ours. Is he going to be okay?" He pointed to the officer laying on an examining table.

"He didn't fare as well as you did. His jaw is broken. He won't be on the bridge for a few weeks."

They were going to drug her again. Whitney knew it was going to happen. It was a risk she had to take to contact Blake. Cortez had threatened to drug her earlier if she tried anything. She had to try to get him to reconsider. "You don't have to do this again. I promise to behave."

He rubbed his chin and smirked. "No. Give her the drug."

Hope faded instantly.

The man with the gun pressed the barrel to the back of her head so she couldn't move.

Then the doctor injected the drug into the muscle of her arm.

"How long will she be out?"

"Long enough for you to get her off the ship and be on your way."

The room spun, and her head flopped to one side. Her muscles felt weak and watery like soup.

All Whitney heard before she passed out was a male voice say, "We've got company—a helicopter."

❈ ❈ ❈

Concern lines raked Captain Dabon's forehead. "The helicopter has circled twice. We don't have much time."

"What about the military ship?"

"It turned east. It's about eighty miles away from us. It must have been doing military manoeuvres like you said."

The helicopter was a problem. A huge problem. Cortez imagined it was the former FBI agent swooping in to rescue his woman. That wasn't going to happen.

After he'd learned that Whitney had made a phone call, crew members had thoroughly cleaned the cabin where Cortez had kept her, including replacing the bloodstained sofa. One of the many advantages of being at sea. Toss whatever you don't want or what you don't want others to know about over the side. Any remnants of the attack earlier had disappeared.

Cortez reached behind the chair and removed the handcuffs from Whitney's wrists and shoved the cuffs and key in his pocket. He scooped up the unconscious woman in his arms. "We must hurry and get her back into the crate."

"What about you?"

"I'll hide in there too. Once I'm inside place some of those other boxes on top." He pointed to the doctor. "Get those oxygen tanks and my duffel bag."

Dabon hurried and pulled the crate out from against the wall. He grunted as he slid the lid off and leaned it against a stack of supplies.

Cortez bent and laid Whitney inside along with her purse. He rolled her onto her side and straightened her legs. Good thing she was not a large woman otherwise he'd be forced to find somewhere else to hide on the ship which would increase his odds of getting caught.

The doctor placed an oxygen tank at the top and the other one at the bottom by the woman's feet. He turned the flow control valve on. The tank hissed on.

Cortez climbed inside the crate and laid down on his side. The fit was tight, especially with the woman beside him and his duffel bag stuffed behind his knees. It would have to work. He hoped he wouldn't be in the cramped space too long.

"I'll turn on the radio. That should drown out the noise from the tanks running." The doctor hurried to the shelf above the examining table and on turned on the radio. Country music filtered through the room. "What about him?"

"Leave him." Cortez looked at the officer on the table. "He's out cold anyway. If anyone asks, tell them he fell on the deck during the storm."

❋ ❋ ❋

Blake cursed under his breath. "The weather's moving in fast." The wind had picked up even more and that had him worried. His pulse drummed in his ears to the same beat as the rotor blades. He didn't need to be slammed into something on the deck. A hit could seriously injury or kill him.

The helicopter's blades tore into the night sky and veered to the left then flew a wide circle around the ship.

"You're going to have to be quick. I'll drop you guys then land on top of the containers. Signal me when you're ready to leave."

Blake lowered the visor on his flight helmet to shield out the driving rain and wind. He and Hal checked their weapons then tugged on their leather gloves with double-thick palms and fingers. They shoved their guns into a pocket of their cargo pants.

Mike did the final test of their rappel hookup, checking the rappel ring and anchor point connection. When he was done he gave them a thumbs-up.

"We're coming around in five," the pilot said.

The helicopter came up fast on the container ship. Rain pelted on the chopper's window and sounded like ricocheting shrapnel. Adrenaline rushed through his body at the thought of bringing Whitney home.

The chopper lowered and hovered. Its spotlight shone down, exposing the dangers below. The ocean was full of rage the way the waves crashed over the railing of the ship and spilled across the deck.

"You're a go. Good luck," the pilot shouted over the rumble of the engine.

With both hands, Mike slid open the side door.

The thump of the main rotor overhead pounded in the wind. The helicopter leaned left then right then finally leveled.

Blake and Hall tossed their rope deployment bags containing extra guns and ammunition out the door away from the helicopter and watched to ensure the ropes didn't land between the landing skids and the chopper or get tangled up. The ropes touched the deck and swayed back and forth like a pendulum on the clock.

They sat in the open door and swung their legs outside the helicopter. Pivoting on the skid they kept their feet spread shoulder-length apart, their knees locked. Sideways rain beat at their pants and nylon jackets.

Blake looked at Hal and he gave him the hand signal that he was ready.

Mike nodded. "Go."

Blake flexed his knees and thrust away from the skid

gear. The rope passed through his brake and guide hand as he descended. Hal descended beside him. His rope swung and spun and he almost knocked into Blake but was able to regain control.

When their feet hit the deck, they crouched to keep from being knocked over from the wind and the down-draft from the chopper. After clearing the rappel ropes through the rappel rings the helicopter's side door swung shut and the chopper flew west.

Hal snatched one of the deployment bags and flung it over his shoulder.

Blake pushed the visor down on his helmet and grabbed the other bag just in time before it started to slide down the deck toward the back of the ship.

The two men hurried to the stairs and ducked under-neath the steel steps for cover from the elements. At times it was difficult for Blake to hear the helicopter's en-gine in the distance due to the howling wind and rain.

They didn't have much more time.

Hal set the bag down and opened it. He retrieved a loaded shotgun then zipped up the bag. "The bridge first?"

"Yeah. Let's do it." Blake pulled out his Glock and thumbed the safety.

As they headed up the stairs, Hal walked ahead of Blake.

On the third landing, Hal stopped and leveled the shotgun.

Rain pounded against Blake's flight helmet and trickled down the back of his neck. A chill spiked up his spine. He looked up at the shadows moving above them within the well-lit bridge.

Hal continued up the stairs, while Blake scanned

below to make sure no one was coming up behind them. In a perfect scenario, he would normally be able to hear the footsteps. This was far from a perfect scenario. They had at least three strikes against them. Maybe more. Each putting Whitney's life at risk. The storm. The unknown. Lack of time to thoroughly search the ship due to the weather. And he had no idea how many crew members they were up against. This was another one of those times he'd be forced to wing it and see how it all played out.

Outside the bridge door, Hal put his bag behind him and crouched. He whispered into his mic. "I see three. The captain and two other crew members."

Blake set his bag down, unzipped it, and grabbed three sets of handcuffs and flipped up his visor. He flattened against the door and peeked in the corner of the window. They weren't big men nor did they look very threatening. He didn't see Whitney or her kidnapper. He held up his fingers. One...two...three...

Hal jumped to his feet and kicked open the door with such force it flew off its hinges.

Blake burst inside and two-handed his gun.

The captain reached for a box on a desk.

Hal raised the shotgun and pointed at the man. "Don't even try it."

"You two over there," Blake directed with the gun.

The two men dressed in black slowly raised their hands and backed up against the wall next to a bank of dozens of knobs and dials.

The captain got out of his chair. "Who are you people? Pirates? We aren't carrying anything of value. Mainly dry goods."

Blake didn't have time for games. "You know damn

well who we are. Where's Cortez and the woman?"

The man folded his arms across his chest and stared at him. "I have no idea what you're talking about. There is no one here by that name and if there was a woman on board, I would be the first to know."

Hal strutted to the captain, stood in front of him, and pointed the barrel of the shotgun in the man's face.

The man didn't even twitch. Blake knew by the defiant expression on the captain's face he wasn't going to give up Whitney.

"We need to get out of here soon," Mike's voice boomed through his headset. "The weather is getting brutal."

Which meant they didn't have time to check the whole ship. Steel bands of panic built in Blake's chest and threatened to cut off the air in his lungs. He gasped for a breath. He had to find Whitney. Time was running out. He knew the chopper couldn't handle the high winds much longer. He couldn't give up. Not yet. "Copy that." Aware that modern container ships like this had autopilot, he tossed two sets of handcuffs to Hal who secured the two men in black while Blake handcuffed the captain to what looked like a steering wheel. He turned to the captain. "How many more on board?"

"Sixteen."

"Where?"

Blake pressed the barrel of his Glock against the man's temple. "I said where?"

"In the engineering room mainly."

He pressed the gun a little harder. "Where are the living quarters, kitchen—"

"Everything is two floors below the bridge." The captain winced. "There's an elevator through there." His eyes shifted to a door painted red at the other end of the bridge.

Confident the men were secure and not going any-where, Blake turned to Hal. "Let's move."

After retrieving their bags and taking the elevator two floors down, Blake and Hal jogged down the hallway weaving in and out of each room searching for Whitney. Not a soul in sight until they checked a small room that appeared to be the infirmary. Inside, a man who appeared to be in his mid-fifties with short gray hair and a well-trimmed beard sat at a desk reading a medical magazine. Country music hummed throughout the room.

The man looked up at Hal's shotgun and then at Blake. He set the magazine down on this knee. "What the hell is going on here?"

The hairs on the back of his neck stirred. Why did Blake get the feeling the man wasn't surprised to see them?

To the right, cardboard and wooden boxes labeled supplies were stacked next to a row of four lockers.

Blake's earpiece rattled. "We got to get off these containers. The wind's going to rip apart the chopper if we don't. The pilot says you've got ten minutes. The weather service just issued a tropical storm warning. Sorry, man."

Hal glanced at him and frowned.

"Roger." Blake clenched his jaw. God damn it! That wasn't long enough. "Where's Cortez and the woman?" He went to the lockers and flung them open one by one. He kept his gun raised while Hal continued to aim the shotgun at the man. The steel doors clanked together and grated against Blake's nerves.

"I'm the doctor. I've been sailing on this ship for fifteen years. I don't know anyone by the name of Cortez and there aren't any women passengers or crew members."

Blake didn't believe him. His response sounded too scripted. The guy knew something. He walked to the other side of the room where a man laid on an examining table with a blanket pulled up to his waist. "What's wrong with him?"

"Took a nasty fall on deck. Smacked his face and head. He's a greenhorn. Been on the ship for less than a week. Some people aren't built to be on a freighter, especially in weather like this."

Blake still didn't believe a word he said. The unconscious man's face looked more like he'd received a kick in the jaw. The outline of the heel of a shoe, complete with tread marks, was etched into his right jaw and cheek.

Whitney was here somewhere.

The ceiling lights flickered.

Blake was running out of time. The storm was beginning to affect the ship. He reached and grabbed the doctor by the shoulder and yanked him to his feet. "Where the hell are they? I'm not asking again." The tone of his voice was a growl, his patience nonexistent.

The doctor stared at him with deadpan eyes. "I don't know what you're talking about."

If Blake thought beating the hell out of the man would help, he'd do it. Anything to help find Whitney. But he knew the guy wasn't going to tell him where she was. "I will be back. And next time I'm not going to be so nice. I'm going to rip your limbs one by one from your body. You can count on it." He shoved the doctor back down in the chair and looked at Hal. "We're wasting time. He isn't going to tell us."

"Wait." The doctor looked at the floor and then up at him. "Another helicopter came. They took her away and the man. They said if I said anything they would kill me and my wife. I know. I'm a doctor. I'm supposed to help people but I couldn't do anything to stop them."

Blake narrowed his eyes and stared at the man, trying to decide if he should believe him or not. The tone of his voice sounded sincere but that didn't mean much especially after Blake had threatened to come back and rip him apart. A desperate man would say anything.

In the hallway, reality hit him like a dozen punishing kicks in the gut. Blake raised his fist and punched the wall leaving a gaping hole in the paneling. He heard Mike's voice in his earpiece but couldn't make out what he was saying.

Hal's put his hand on his shoulder. "The doc could be telling the truth."

Blake rubbed his forehead. He could stay here and thoroughly search the ship. But that could take days with a ship this size. He needed to make a decision. Part of the doctor's story made sense. Taking Whitney off the ship would continue Pablo's quest to get Blake on his own turf in Colombia exactly where he wanted him for the final showdown.

"Let's move before the helicopter is torn apart by the storm."

Hal nodded then they ran down the hallway to the elevator.

CHAPTER FOURTEEN

Two hours after leaving the *TransVenture*, Blake returned home exhausted and emotionally drained. Whitney's phone call played over in his head.

"Blake, they're taking me to Pablo Sanchez."

In the bedroom, he quickly stuffed some clothes into a duffel bag. His chest hurt. The deep ache had developed the second Whitney had been kidnapped. He missed her more than he'd ever admit to anyone. He didn't like leaving the freighter not knowing for sure if she was on board or not. If the doctor had lied and she was still on the ship, according to the manifest it would be two days before she arrived at the port in Tumaco and Blake, Mike, and Hal would be there waiting.

As he finished packing, Whitney's fearful words continued to haunt him. He'd walk to the end of the earth to save her.

Traveling in Colombia with a bounty on his head would prove challenging and extremely dangerous if not deadly. Everyone would know he was coming. Pablo would make sure of it. It was all part of the game.

Even though Mike and Hal had offered to go with him, Blake needed more help—assistance within the country.

He only trusted one man; Oscar Moreno, a veteran cop, a captain with the Colombian National Police. He was one of the good guys, one of the few whose life hadn't be tainted by dirty cartel money.

At last estimate, the DEA approximated that the majority working within the National Police were on the Sur del Calle's payroll receiving anywhere from fifteen to fifteen thousand dollars a week to ensure Sanchez's drug and weapons business ran smoothly. With an established network across the US, in particular businesses like travel agencies and small independently run stores to serve as money laundering fronts used to wire transfer large amounts of cash, channeling hundreds of millions of dollars back into Colombia was the lifeblood of the cartel. Without the money Sanchez and the cartel received from the US and other countries they couldn't manufacture, distribute, or transport their deadly goods.

If anyone could help Blake get into the country without any problems it would be Oscar. The cop had been there for him over a decade ago deep in the jungle overlooking Bogotá during an undercover mission that went south. Mike and Blake were working with four DEA agents trying to nail Pablo Sanchez when his twin brother, Manuel, learned that Blake and Mike were FBI agents. Oscar and his team came in hard just in time, with guns blazing, giving Blake the opportunity to kill Manuel seconds before he planned to execute Mike. If Pablo ever learned Moreno and his men had been involved, not only would they be dead, so would their families. The guy had saved Mike's life and probably Blake's as well.

He grabbed the duffel bag off the bed and shut off the bedroom light. He'd call Oscar on the way to the airport.

They'd have to come up with a plan.

Cortez's eyes readjusted to the bright ceiling lights as he stepped out of the crate. He hated being in there. It felt as if he had been buried alive. He looked at the woman sleeping. He didn't know what the doctor had injected into her but Cortez couldn't keep drugging her. Next time she might not wake up. If she didn't, Pablo would not be happy.

"They left. The weather scared them off," the doctor said. "I had to tell them a bullshit story that a helicopter took you and the woman off the ship earlier after one of the men threatened he would be back."

Probably Blake Barnett. The woman's fiancé.

He walked to the fridge, opened it, and took out a bottle of water. His whole face, especially his nose, throbbed and a headache hammered at the back of his head. He winced. "I need more painkillers."

The doctor opened the medical kit and tossed him a bottle of medication.

He caught the bottle and popped two pills into his mouth, downing them with a gulp of cold water.

Cortez had no idea how Blake Barnett discovered the name of the ship. He should never have been on the *TransVenture*. Everyone including himself had been so careful. Pablo needed to be notified—and he wasn't going to be happy.

❋ ❋ ❋

Pablo stood shirtless and barefoot outside the sprawling lit enclosure and watched one of his men toss a wild boar down the long steel chute. The Bengal tiger pounced, its teeth ripping at the carcass as she dragged the meat across the dirt until she settled in the corner. A light warm breeze vibrated the palm trees surrounding the compound. The tiger froze for a second then continued tearing the meat from the boar's bones. She pawed her foot across the dirt and then roared, happy with her dinner. Pablo was surprised the cat was still hungry after devouring Taliana hours before. The only remnants of the young woman's short existence—four or five long bones and her skull which the tiger playfully batted around on the grass in the late afternoon sun.

Alejandro stood beside Pablo with his hands tucked behind his back. Lights lit a narrow path down the Monserrate Mountains behind them. The man appeared to be in deep thought, mourning the loss of Raul and Enzo. He looked smaller tonight. Frown lines appeared deeper around his mouth in the moonlight. Pablo knew what it was like to lose someone he cared about. He missed his brother. Manuel would be standing here right now if it wasn't for Blake Barnett.

As they walked back to the house, Eduardo was leaning against the house smoking a cigar. Four other of Pablo's most trusted men were scattered around the terrace and pool. Below, the city—his city—was alive with its skyscrapers and homes with terracotta roofs financed with the cartel's money.

Pablo's cell phone rang. He dug into his pants pocket and answered the call. "Hola."

"It's Cortez. The American ship is no longer a threat. We will arrive on time in Tumaco."

"Perfect." The hairs on Pablo's arms prickled. Cortez's voice sounded strained. "Is there a problem?"

"It's Barnett. He found out which ship we were on. He

came searching for the woman."

Pablo's pulse sped up. He held the phone in a death grip, his fingers ready to snap in half. "Do you still have the woman?"

"Yes, I had her hidden well. No one would have found her."

Someone had opened their mouth about his plan. Whoever it was, they were dead. Pablo had killed for less, so much less. "How did he find out?"

"I don't know."

Pablo wiped the sweat from his forehead. His stomach soured. "Find out. Then kill them."

CHAPTER FIFTEEN

Fourteen hours and three stopovers later Blake, Mike, and Hal landed at the coastal La Florida Airport in Tumaco at nine fifteen in the morning.

Blake wasn't happy about taking a commercial flight, but their cover needed to be believable. Three American business men looking to invest some major cash into a downtown Bogotá building project. Chambers had met them last night at McCarran Airport with their new passports complete with updated photos and new names. As of today, Blake's new name was Jackson Davis.

Three days had passed since Cortez kidnapped Whitney and the *TransVenture* would arrive early tomorrow. Blake knew they couldn't just walk onto the ship when it docked unless they wanted to be arrested or worse. Details needed to be worked out with the help of his friend, Oscar.

Inside the airport, Blake stood in the Customs line and watched as Mike and Hal's passports were scrutinized. The Custom's officer was a tall woman maybe in her early thirties dressed in two-tone green camouflage shirt and pants. When it was his turn, he stepped up to the counter and gave the agent his passport.

While she took her time checking it, he filled out and signed a Declaration of Baggage and Currency form used to report personal effects, including the amount of currency he was bringing into the country. As if anyone would declare they were bringing large sums of money into the country.

When the agent handed back his passport, he looked up and she smiled.

His attention snapped directly behind her. Pinned to a bulletin board cluttered with paper was a wanted poster with his face on it.

Blake's heart stopped. Being hunted was not a game he wanted to play. The sooner he got out of the airport the better. The last place he wanted to end up was in a hellhole of a Colombian prison or dead.

Play it cool. He took his passport. "Gracias."

After claiming their bags, Blake walked behind Mike and Hal not wanting to appear in a rush. Anything to divert attention from himself. By the way, the guys were chatting back and forth it was clear they had spotted the poster too. One thing Blake had learned from many years of undercover work with the Bureau, people always noticed other's talking to each other before they noticed a person alone. Humans were nosy and curious and more apt to divert their attention to people talking loudly, allowing Blake the chance to fly under the radar.

At the other end of the airport, the flight waiting area didn't look much different than Blake remembered from over a decade ago. Just a couple extra thick coats of beige paint and a few new pieces of artwork in vibrant shades of pink, yellow, and blue on the walls. The three men strolled through the small lounge fitted with about twenty uncomfortable looking metal chairs and then walked straight out the front door.

Outside, Blake exhaled a sigh of relief. So far so good.

Seeing the wanted poster made things all too real. He kept on walking.

The once dirt parking lot had been replaced with paving stones and was landscaped throughout with orchids and pink flowering bushes. Wax palm trees waved in the briny Pacific air and provided much needed shade from the heated morning sun. A yellow tented picnic area with tables constructed from wooden slats was empty. The structure didn't appear as if it had been used in quite some time.

Oscar said he'd send someone to pick them up and take them to an undisclosed location then meet him there. Blake understood why the man didn't want to be seen in public with them. He didn't want a target on his back. He couldn't put his family in danger in case any of Pablo's men recognized Blake or Mike. They were all risking their lives to save Whitney.

The lot was almost barren except for three red motorcycles and a well-used silver pickup truck parked with its engine running—their ride.

After tossing their duffel bags into the bed of the pickup, Blake opened the passenger door and got in. Mike and Hal climbed into the back seat and closed the doors.

The male driver shot Blake a smile. "Hola. I'm Juan. Oscar sent me."

"Thanks for picking us up." Blake glanced at the parking lot area still on high alert after spotting the wanted poster.

Juan nodded. He threw the truck in reverse, stopped, and then put the vehicle into drive.

Blake didn't know if the guy was a police officer or just a friend of Oscar's. Whoever the man was, Blake appreciated the risk he was taking.

At the entrance of the airport parking lot, two stocky guards dressed in military fatigues armed with AK-47s walked back and forth across the first of many checkpoints Blake was positive they would encounter along the way.

As their driver steered the truck down the road, the pickup bounced and weaved through a maze of orange metal pylons and chunks of battered white concrete used as speed barriers around the airport.

Blake clutched the dashboard. His body bopped up and down, his head hitting the roof of the truck with each jolt. He glanced over his shoulder at Mike and Hal hanging on for dear life. Six-foot wooden fences with razor wire at the top were erected on both sides of the road for at least an eighth of a mile. Once they were out of the protected area the driver gunned the engine.

Tumaco had always been a highly valued location for the cartel, filled with a wealth of rivers, in particular, the Mira River that ran into the sea. The perfect passageway for delivering drugs and weapons to ships which would later sail on to Ecuador, Mexico, and the United States.

Three motorcycles whizzed by in the opposite lane and sounded more like lawn mowers than motorbikes. Every few minutes Blake glanced in the side-view mirror to make sure they weren't being followed. A compact taxi cab painted bright yellow followed close behind them. He leaned his head back on the headrest and thought about Whitney.

Regardless of what the ship's doctor had said, Blake wasn't convinced she had been removed from the *Trans-Venture* by helicopter. He didn't buy it. She was on that damn ship. He could feel it. But how the hell was he going to rescue her? The port would be infested with the military and Pablo's men. Worst case scenario, he'd be forced to wait until she was off the ship to make his move. Blake didn't like what he was up against.

Too many obstacles. Too many unknowns. Too many men with guns.

Twenty minutes later the driver slowed the truck and steered down a long driveway off the main road. Stones crunched under the tires. He parked at the side of a large white house with a blue tin roof and shut off the ignition.

He looked at Blake. "Oscar will meet you here. He said there's food and everything else you will need inside." He handed him a key. "I'll wait here until he arrives."

"Thanks." Blake took the key and got out of the truck.

Hal and Mike exited the vehicle and grabbed their duffel bags and headed toward the front door of the house.

Blake scooped his bag out of the bed of the pickup and scanned the area. The house was located on a low traffic street with lots of green space separating the neighbors, and it was overlooking the bay. Behind the structure, he spotted four large freight vessels being escorted into the harbor. To the east, two tall cranes towered over the port's terminal, exactly where the *TransVenture* would be docking in less than seventeen hours.

Once inside the house, Blake looked around the living room. A plush chocolate brown couch and matching chair shared a scratched and stained wooden coffee table between them. An older model television complete with knobs to change the channels and adjust the volume sat on a book shelf in the corner of the room. A laptop, printer, camera, and other electronic equipment was spread out on a makeshift desk constructed from dented metal file cabinets at each end with a long plank of wood set on top. The place wasn't anything fancy but comfortable.

Mike dropped his bag on the beaten gold linoleum floor next to the couch. "Looks like a Colombian version of a US safe house. It's even got a steel front door."

Hal opened one of the drapes. "There's bars on the windows too." He tapped on the glass and smiled. "Nice. One and a half inch bullet resistant Plexiglass."

"We should be safe." At least until someone learns we're here. Blake prayed that wouldn't happen because he had to find Whitney and get her safely out of the country. At the moment they didn't have an exit plan and that worried him. Once Whitney was safe, how were they going to get out of the country?

"Hoping that doesn't happen too soon. I'm going to see what we've got for food and conjure us up some breakfast." Hal walked past them and headed to the kitchen.

Blake's stomach growled. It was actually the first time since Whitney had been kidnapped that he was hungry. The lukewarm watered-down airport coffee he'd grabbed before they left Las Vegas wasn't going to cut it.

While Mike checked out the laptop and other electronic toys, Blake wandered down a hallway to a bedroom with two single beds and a six-drawer dresser. He set his bag on one of the beds.

In a second bedroom, there were two more single-sized beds with a half dozen folded army green colored blankets stacked on each. A spacious bathroom complete with a shower was directly across the hall. After using the washroom, he went back to the living room.

Mike was still at the desk pecking away on the laptop and printing out maps they would need of the Tumaco port.

Hal set a plate of food beside Mike and then handed Blake a heaping platter of scrambled eggs and two slices of toast.

"Thanks." Blake took a seat on the sofa and ate.

When he finished devouring his food he set the empty plate on the coffee table. "That was great. I think Mike and I need to have you come along on all of our little adventures."

Hal laughed. "Well let's hope to hell this is the last adventure you have with Pablo Sanchez and friends."

It would be.

Blake would make sure of it.

A knock on the door made all the men scramble. Everyone's nerves were on edge. Mike stood on one side of the door while Hal took position on the other side and waited. Without any weapons, they were sitting ducks.

Blake went to the window and peeked through the curtains to see Oscar stop and talk to Juan briefly. Juan then got into the pickup and backed out of the driveway.

His muscles relaxed. "It's Oscar."

Mike unlocked the door and opened it.

Oscar walked inside.

The forty-eight-year-old man looked as if he had barely aged in over a decade other than a few more gray hairs threading his thick black hair and mustache. Oscar was bull-necked, squat, and could be mean as hell. Being a police captain in a country with so much violence, he had to be. Not the kind of guy you would want to take on unless you wanted to lose. They didn't call him Oscar the Bull for no reason.

His brown eyes sparkled as he grinned at Mike. "It's good to see you. How have you been?"

"I've been good. Staying out of trouble." Mike shook the man's hand. "It's been too long, my friend." He pointed to Hal. "This is Hal Decker. He was in the Marines with us."

Hal shook Oscar's hand with both hands. "Nice to meet you. The guys speak highly of you. Any friend of theirs is a friend of mine."

Oscar patted Hal on the shoulder then turned to Blake. "It's great to see you, but I'm sorry you're here under these circumstances."

Blake was too. He shook Oscar's hand, the same hand that'd saved his and Mike's lives in the jungle so long ago. He had nothing but respect for the man. "How's your wife and daughter?"

"Mariana is doing well. She still works as a nurse and runs the medical clinic here in Tumaco. My daughter, Sofia, is in her first year in college studying food and restaurant management. She hopes when she's done school that she can secure an internship in the United States."

Pride shone in his friend's eyes as he spoke about his family. "That's fantastic, Oscar. Thanks for the place to stay. It's very much appreciated."

"I want nothing more than to help you get Whitney back. I saw the wanted posters being circulated. They're everywhere. This is going to be difficult. It appears Pablo is doing everything he can to make sure he gets you. It's my unofficial job to make sure that doesn't happen. Let me show you something." Oscar headed down the hallway to the second bedroom.

Blake, Mike, and Hal followed.

Oscar rolled up an area rug on the floor then pulled the bed out from the wall. In the floor was a square of torn and tattered linoleum about four feet in diameter.

He pressed his foot on the right corner of the square and a door sprung open. A metal ladder was visible in the diffused light from the window.

"Well, I'll be damned. This place is a safe house," Hal said.

"It's my Colombian casa de seguridad. I'm sure much different than a US one. It has been here for about twenty years. No one knows about it. Not Pablo or his men. If all hell breaks loose in this country this is where I will be with my family. Come on. I think you'll be surprised."

Once they were all down, Oscar turned on a light.

Surprised was an understatement.

Blake was sure his mouth was gaping open much like Hal's and Mike's.

On one side of the room, open boxes of weapons were stacked eight feet high. Row after row of pistols, assault rifles, machine guns, tons of ammunition. The side shelves were filled with food. It reminded Blake of the bomb shelters built in the fifties except no one would ever have the sheer number of weapons present here.

Hal had a goofy grin on his face as if he'd been dropped in the middle of a weapons factory. "What have you been doing? Stockpiling for a war?"

"These are leftovers from many wars between the military, police, cartel, and a number of paramilitary and militia groups."

Mike picked up a Beretta and then an M16A2 rifle. "Guess this solves our lack of weapons issue."

Blake was relieved they had an arsenal of guns at their disposal if needed. "What's your friend Juan's story?"

"Juan is an informant. He's been helping me for many years."

"Can we trust him?"

"I have no reason not to." Oscar paused for a moment before continuing. "About eight years ago, Pablo slaughtered his wife and five-year-old son because Juan refused to run drugs for the cartel. He runs for them now but not by choice. He wants to see Sanchez pay for his crimes."

He wasn't the only one. Revenge was a powerful motivator when loved ones were involved. Blake knew that all too well.

After they headed back up to the living room, Oscar flattened one of the maps Mike had printed out earlier onto the center of the coffee table. "There's a hill right here. You can see the docks from there." He pointed to the spot on the map and then looked up at Blake. "It's on the north side of a dirt road that the cartel uses. We'll need to stay hidden and be extremely careful."

"What time does the *TransVenture* arrive?"

"ETA is one in the morning," Mike said.

Blake glanced at his watch. They had a good twelve hours to wait.

"What's the plan? Do we grab her once she's off the ship?" Hal asked.

Oscar's eyes shifted to Hal. "It will depend on how many men are guarding the dock. Each night is different. I think it's safe to assume there will be a heavier presence considering something valuable is coming in— something they've been told is extremely important to Pablo."

Blake nodded. "I agree. We're going to have play wait and see on this one. Oscar, can you get your hands on some night vision binoculars? We're going to need them."

"Of course. I'm sure I have whatever we need in the underground bunker as you call it and whatever I don't have, I will go get."

Blake was pretty sure his friend did since it appeared he had everything else. "You don't have to come with us, Oscar. We certainly understand if you don't want to. I don't want you to put your family in any danger."

He put his hand on Blake's forearm. "I'm a police offi-cer first. The choice is mine. You need my knowledge of the country to assist in rescuing Whitney. I would like nothing more than to see Pablo and his closest comrades pay with their lives for what they have done—to the country and to all Colombians."

❊ ❊ ❊

After most of the crew had left the ship other than a couple men still in the engineering room, Cortez stayed behind on the bridge to call his wife.

Whitney Steel was loaded into the truck and was still sleeping in the crate. Soon she would wake and find her-self traveling through the jungle to Pablo's compound.

The plan changed once the former FBI agent had dis-covered their travel plans. Cortez wasn't going to take a chance and travel by train. Not now. Blake Barnett was smart. He had no idea who had revealed the ship's name to him, but someone had a big mouth. Maybe it was Luis Silva or his brother-in-law the harbor cop. If so, they wouldn't be alive for long. No one went against Pablo Sanchez's orders and lived. No one.

With a new plan in place, Cortez felt confident the last part of his journey with the woman would be trouble free. Nothing like what he'd experienced so far—killing Raul and Enzo and then beating the hell out of him. The woman was trouble and he couldn't wait to be free of her and return home to his wife and sons.

He rubbed his forehead. The back of his skull and nose throbbed and pulsated to an imaginary drum beat in his head. She wouldn't get another opportunity to attack him again.

His decision to drive eighteen hours instead of taking the train gave him another advantage—added protection since the majority of police and military between Tumaco and Bogotá were on Pablo's payroll.

Cortez pulled the throw-away cell phone from his knapsack and called his wife at the restaurant. After four rings he heard her tired voice on the other end of the line.

"The Cocina. Good morning. This is Isabella."

"Buenos días, mi amor. I miss you. I will be home in three days. How are our sons?"

"It's you. How dare you call me. They said you kidnapped that reporter—the one on the news and shot a man. Is this true?"

Cortez shook his head. He felt as if the wind had been knocked out of him. How did she know? "I have not kidnapped anyone, Isabella." He forced himself to laugh. "Who told you such silliness?"

"The FBI. They were here at our restaurant asking if I knew where you were. They said you have that woman and you are giving her to Pablo Sanchez. Why would you do this? Why, Cortez? We both know what the man will do. He's killed many of our people."

A wall of panic hit him in the middle of his stomach as if someone had reached in and twisted, cutting off the air to his lungs. "What did you say to them, Isabella—to the FBI agent?"

"Is it true, Cortez? Did you kidnap that woman?"

What would his sons think of him when they learned the truth? Their father a kidnapper...

"Tell me." His voice turned hard doused with fear, and he yelled at his wife, something he never did, something he was taught not to do. "Please tell me what you said to them. It's important."

"I said you were on a buying trip for spices like you always do. They asked me about a ship called the *Trans-Venture*. I told them I heard the name when you and Raul were speaking on the phone."

It was her. His own wife. She was the one. Pablo had ordered him to kill whoever was responsible for leaking the information. How could he go against a man he'd known all his life?

He paced in a small circle trying to comprehend what she said and what he was going to do. He couldn't kill his wife. He loved her. Nor could he go back to his life in the United States. Not now. Not ever. Isabella had no idea what she'd done.

It didn't matter that Cortez and Pablo had been friends since they were children. If his boss discovered it was his wife who'd given the information about the ship to Blake Barnett, Pablo would kill her as well as his sons. He did not tolerate disloyalty.

"Isabella, it's not safe. You're all in danger. Get on a plane and go anywhere. Not to Colombia. Don't ask questions. Just do it."

❊ ❊ ❊

Blake lay on his stomach and peered through the green haze of the night vision binoculars at the *Trans-Venture* docked in the offshore berth in Tumaco Bay. Insects trilled and played their own personal anthem. Their presence rattled him. He didn't like bugs, especially big creepy ugly ones. Much like he didn't like cats.

It had taken him years to get over his fear of the purring furry creatures all thanks to Whitney and her love for all animals. The closer he got to rescuing her the more he missed her. The ship had arrived three hours ago and still no sign of her. His jaw tightened. Where was she?

At four o'clock in the morning, light rain fell as cranes worked through the night lifting the metal containers off the ship and transferring them into the terminal.

Hal lay next to him with his binoculars aimed at the ship. Mike and Oscar were crouched a few feet away under a canopy of trees studying the significant military presence below.

Hal shimmied on his belly with his elbows a few feet through the dense vegetation and pushed aside one of the bushes. "Looks like about three dozen soldiers, including Colombian Navy Special Forces. I count eight with dogs."

Small birds chirped. Branches swished overhead and at times it sounded as if someone was sneaking up behind them. Half the time it was difficult to know where the different noises were originating from.

"There's also a dozen police officers. I'm ashamed to say most of them are probably on Pablo Sanchez's payroll," Oscar said as he swatted an insect off his cheek.

He heard the repugnance in his friend's voice. Blake was just as disgusted. With Tumaco close to the border of Ecuador, crime ran rampant. Police, army, gangs, traffickers, paramilitary groups, guerrillas, and militias were all fighting for control. With control came money. Lots of it. Especially if you were on the cartel's payroll—but many people didn't have a choice. Most Colombians were just trying to keep themselves and their loved ones alive. They had to take money from the cartel which made Blake wonder how Oscar had survived this long without being on the take.

Something slithered in the tall grass in front of him. Blake shifted and moved backwards. Dead leaves crunched, the smell of wet dirt mixed with ocean air and fresh rain.

Mike stood then peeked over the embankment. "Southwest corner of the terminal. Two Humvees with machine guns parked with their headlights on. I don't see any way in without sounding the alarm. There's too many of them."

Blake agreed. It was too risky. He mopped the rain from his face with the sleeve of his shirt and continued to view the dock area. Fourteen male crew members including the captain and doctor had already disembarked from the ship. Four other men were busy loading boxes and wooden crates into an army green colored box van. A nervous sweat prickled on his back. "Where the hell is she?"

"The ship's doc might have been telling the truth all along," Hal said.

Blake detected concern in Hal's voice. He set the binoculars down. If she wasn't on the ship then she was already on her way to Pablo or the bastard already had her. His heart pounded in his chest, choking him. He'd seen what Sanchez did to women and children just for fun. He needed to get to her before it was too late.

"If we don't spot Whitney by sunrise we're going to have to meet Pablo on his own turf."

Whitney woke with a jolt. She was sick and tired of her captor drugging her. The last image in her mind was the ship's doctor injecting her with something. Her body didn't feel weak and exhausted like the last time. Whatever he'd given her was different than she'd experienced when she had woken up on the ship. Her hair was still pulled back in a ponytail and she was wearing the same jogging suit she had on when she attacked Cortez on the ship. Both a good sign that nothing horrible had happened to her.

Why didn't Blake come for me? Panic rose deep within her and seeped through her body and threatened to strangle her. She'd called him. That much she remembered.

She sat in the middle of the bench seat squished between Cortez and another man who smelled strongly of body odor and cigarette smoke. The smell almost gagged her. Her wrists were handcuffed. A long chain looped through the cuffs and was secured to the door handle. Her captor had learned his lesson. He wasn't taking any chances this time. Getting out of this one might prove to be difficult. At least her feet weren't bound.

Cortez clutched the steering wheel with both hands, his face swollen and red. The skin beneath both eyes was puffy and a rainbow of blues, black, and purple. The army type vehicle they were driving in was much like a pickup truck but longer and wider with a canvas cover on the back. She peered out the dusty and dirty windshield at the brilliant colored foliage along the road. Vibrant green covered mountains rose up on both sides of the meandering road.

He turned his head and shot her a smirk. "Don't even think of trying anything or I'll heave you out the door and drag you behind the truck."

By the harsh growl of his voice, Whitney believed he would, especially after what she'd done to his face. A chill raced up her spine and fresh panic set in. She glanced over her shoulder out the back window.

Where was Blake? Why hadn't he come for her? She prayed something hadn't happened to him. Her attention shifted to the men speaking Spanish.

"Deberiamos estar alli en seis horas," Cortez said.

The man beside her nodded his bald head and said, "Seis a lo sumo."

Whitney had no idea what they were talking about other than she knew 'seis' meant six. Six days? Six men? She had no clue. It could mean anything including six hours to live. She erased the horrible thought from her mind and tried to concentrate on figuring out what she was going to do. Besides being tired, hungry, and thirsty, she hadn't seen another human or a house except for an old woman selling vegetables at a roadside stand a few miles back. Being a reporter, Whitney was aware the Colombian jungles were crawling with militias and other deadly groups who raped and murdered because they could. The last thing she wanted was to be a permanent guest of the Revolutionary Armed Forces of Colombia who usually kidnapped for ransom. Americans were not exempt. She would not be exempt. She'd die for sure. For the first time, she felt extremely vulnerable.

Suddenly the truck slowed.

Whitney straightened in the seat and looked out the window.

Two men dressed in two-tone green camouflage uniforms with assault rifles stood at a wooden blockade setup in the center of the road. Military? They couldn't possibly ignore the fact she was tethered to a chain like a dog and leashed to the truck door. How could they? But her captor didn't appear concerned which made her worry. She wrung her hands in her lap. The metal cuffs clanked together. Even if she could escape would she be any better off roaming the wilderness compared to her final destination? Pablo Sanchez was going to kill her. The higher up the mountain they drove, the denser the vegetation became. She sighed. Escaping into the jungle was not an option.

Cortez stopped the truck.

A short, bearded man dressed in crisp fatigues grasping an assault rifle in one hand and with a machete attached to his hip spoke to her captor in Spanish. The man stuck his head inside the window, looked at her, and then back to Cortez.

Please help me. The words stuck to her tongue and her voice deserted her when her captor passed the man a stack of money.

The man waved to the other guard on the road. Moments later the barricade was moved to the side of the road, allowing them access up the mountain.

Cortez glared at her, smiled, and then stomped the accelerator.

Whitney leaned her head against the back of the seat and closed her eyes. Where was Blake? Not knowing was driving her crazy. He said he'd be on the ship. Something happened. Her palms grew damp and her stomach turned into a tight ball. But what? She prayed he would show up soon. Time was running out.

As they drove for hours, the sun lowered behind the mountains and the air turned cooler. The once paved road melted away into a narrow dirt path congested with ruts and bumps. The man beside her didn't say a word as he lit and smoked cigarettes one after another. At times the smoke choked her even with the windows down.

"I really need to go to the bathroom." The thought of stopping on the side of the road didn't appeal to her but she had to go.

Cortez pulled to the shoulder and stopped. "Déjala salir y tener un arma en ella en todo momento."

"Sí." The man beside her bent over and pulled a gun out from under the seat. He pointed it at her then opened the door. The heavy chain tugged the cuffs around her wrists and pulled her arms forward.

Outside the vehicle, Whitney took five steps away from the truck and the chain snapped taut and stopped her from going any farther. She looked over her shoulder to find the man staring at her. "Could I have some privacy?"

"Dé su privacidad, Alvaro."

Whatever Cortez said to the man made him turn his back allowing her to go to the bathroom without him gawking at her. She could knock him out and then yank the chain off the door handle but where would she go? The trees and brush were so thick, not to mention the wild animals and snakes hidden within the jungle. She'd die before she got to help. Whitney pulled up her pants and drew a deep breath. She was going to have to wait and hope Blake showed up before it was too late.

After getting back into the vehicle, they continued to drive higher up the mountain and at times she swore the truck was going to fall over the edge of the narrow road. Evening turned into night and dim headlights swung from one side to the other and up and down each time Cortez dodged a rut in the road.

Whitney stared out the window at the sky speckled with stars winking over the mountains and thought about her father. He was executed in a country overrun with torture and death and she wondered if her destiny would be the same? The deep ache in her heart returned—the horrible empty feeling of the loss of both her parents. At least when she lost her mother Whitney knew why. A drunk driver. Not something a young child accepted or understood, but at least she knew. It was different with her father. After all these years there were still so many unanswered questions. All she was told—he was executed by militants in Colombia. No other details. Years of research and digging left her with more questions than answers. What was he working on?

His last words before he'd left for his last assignment trickled through her thoughts where they would stay etched forever in her mind. "Honey, you can't choose your fate. Fate chooses you."

She glanced at her captor then to the man beside her. Fate might have chosen this path for her and she may not have any control over what might happen once they reached Pablo, but Whitney did have control over what she was going to do about it. She looked at her engagement ring. Newfound strength and determination flooded her body. Survival instinct kicked in stronger than ever. Patience and persistence. With her father watching over her, she had faith the right moment would present itself and she would be free of Pablo Sanchez once and for all.

The truck slowed to almost a full stop then veered left. The dirt road was narrower than the one they'd been on and she wondered if the truck would make the climb. Light from the headlights bounced and jerked off the road and into the trees. Thick foliage scraped against the side of the truck and sounded like a snare brush against a metal drum.

"We're here. Finally, you'll be out of my hands," Cortez said.

Out of his hands and into Pablo's.

Her pulse pounded in her ears. She had no idea what she was going to be walking into.

The end of the road opened to a gigantic area free of thick vegetation. Ornate lampposts lit the driveway leading to a brick mansion situated high on a hill. Ten-foot stone walls with wrought iron fencing attached at the top surrounded the home. Two guards with rifles stood on either side of the twenty-foot-high iron gate.

Cortez steered the truck up to the gate and stopped. Each guard pushed open a side of the gate and her captor drove through and up the long driveway to the garage on the side of the house.

Pablo kept her alive this long for a reason. Whitney had to believe he would keep her alive a bit longer—long enough for her to figure out what she was going to or for Blake to show up. She crossed her fingers in her lap.

Once her captor shut off the ignition, he got out and closed the door. The man beside her exited the vehicle. Cortex unlocked the paddle lock on the chain from the door and gave it a tug. Whitney slid across the seat and out the door.

It was clear he wanted to degrade her by the way he was leading her around on the metal leash for what she had done to his face and to Raul and Enzo.

"Get going. Pablo is waiting." He dragged her by the chain while the other man walked behind her with his gun aimed at her head.

A deep low growl. Then a roar.

Whitney stopped. Her head snapped to the left and then to the right, unsure where the sound came from—or from what.

Cortez jerked the chain and forced her feet to move.

Her legs trembled with each step. What the hell growled? *Please, Blake, find me.*

At the side door of the house, a man greeted her captor. He appeared to be in his sixties with silver hair, his skin deeply tanned, almost black under the light above the three-car garage. He smiled and gave Cortex a quick hug.

"This is her?" The man looked her up and down then pursed his lips. "This is the woman who killed Enzo and Raul?"

"Yes, Alejandro. She is the one. I'm sorry. They were good men and good friends. They will be missed."

The man lifted his hand and touched her captor's face. "She did this to you?"

Cortez glanced at her then back to the man. "Yes."

Alejandro stared at her for a long moment. "You're like your father. You look just like him."

Her father? "What are you talking about? My father is dead."

He remained silent.

What the hell was he talking about? Her father was dead and now this guy was talking as if he was alive. It didn't make sense.

His eyes held an expression intense with hatred. Then he slapped her across the face.

The blow knocked her head to one side and made her face sting with fire. Whitney had no idea who the man was but he wasn't going to hit her again. If he tried, she'd drop-kick him. "Don't touch me again."

His eyes narrowed and he spit at her feet. "Take her inside. Pablo will make sure she pays for killing Enzo and

Raul."

* * *

Sunrise came and went and still no sign of Whitney. They'd waited until an hour after the sun made its appearance and no one else got off the ship. Blake's heartbeat thundered in his chest. He wasn't sure where she was. He just wanted to find her.

Back at the house, he forced himself to eat a hearty breakfast with two cups of coffee, and then paced the living room anxious to get moving. It was eight-thirty and the sooner they got to Whitney the better.

Oscar had left an hour ago to pick up some supplies they needed that he didn't have in his underground bunker including Kevlar vests. He also wanted to switch his vehicle for something more practical for the mission. A vehicle which would fit in better with the Colombian landscape and make them less conspicuous.

They'd have to go to Bogotá where Pablo had the home turf advantage. They didn't have a choice. Creepy big bugs would be the least of their worries.

Blake turned to Mike and Hal sitting on the couch. He cracked his knuckles. "This is it. If anyone wants to back out, I'd understand."

"That's not going to happen," Mike said, then took a sip of his coffee. "I'm not leaving until you have Whitney back."

Hal looked up at Blake and shook his head. "No way, man. We're bringing her home together. We came here together. We leave together. That was the deal. Besides, I want to see Sanchez suffer when he takes his last dying breath, preferably with my hands wrapped around his neck."

"Not if I can get to the prick first." Mike slapped Hal on the back.

Both men would have to wait in line. Blake appreciated the fact his friends weren't going to back down and supported him one hundred percent. "Thanks, guys."

They were all aware of the dangers. So was Blake. They'd been here before. The odds of getting Whitney safely out of the country were slim. Less than twenty percent. He tried not to think about the ratio, determined to move forward with their plan to rescue her.

"Mike, can you contact Chambers and work on an exit plan? Not sure what he can do from his end but we're going to need all the help we can get when it's time to leave."

"Sure. Maybe we can fly out of the same airport we did last time we were here if it hasn't been overrun by paramilitary or worse. I can't remember the name of it, but I'll look into it." He got up off the couch and went to the desk and opened the laptop.

Blake couldn't remember the name of the airport either. He was pretty certain things had changed and the Colombian government allowed American military flights into the country only at designated airports. That might be their ride out.

Hal set the magazine he was reading down on the coffee table next to the maps and the growing collection of empty coffee cups. "What do you want me to do?"

"Gather up what weapons and ammunition you think we'll need from the bunker. We might as well start getting packed up. I think I saw some black knapsacks near the weapons. We can probably use them. When Oscar returns we'll be ready to go."

Hal nodded then disappeared down the hallway to the

bedroom to the secret trap door.

Even though the fastest route to Bogotá was to fly, an hour flight, Blake didn't want to risk using the airport again in case someone outed him as the guy in the wanted poster. He might look a lot different with his new look but it wasn't a chance he was willing to take.

Instead, they would drive northeast by car, an eighteen-hour ride along a stretch of highway. His meal sat heavy in his stomach, reminding him of the countless possible dangers.

They were already right smack in the middle of a wasteland and heading into an even worse area—a hub of criminal activity where people simply disappeared at the hands of violent outlaw groups who settled their differences with guns and sometimes bombs. Many of the port areas in the country were filled with slums, the result of decades of different fractions and gangs fighting for the right to be the top dog. Most of the criminals in the area recruited children, extorted small business owners, and even had casas de pique—chop houses where they tortured and dismembered victims alive, dumping their remains in the bay and the jungle. They could be stopped anytime on the way. It was risky. There sure as hell weren't any guarantees, not in one of the most crime infested countries in South America. He'd do everything in his power to ensure everyone made it out of this alive.

While Mike and Hal worked on their tasks, Blake went and took a long hot shower to clear his head and relax his aching body. Afterward, he slipped on a pair of jeans and pulled a dark green T-shirt over his head. He heard Oscar's voice coming from the living room.

"Look what he brought us." Hal's eyes lit up when Blake walked into the room. "Toys."

Blake eyed the drone on the floor in the middle of the room.

"We've been using this technology to locate cocaine laboratories in the jungle. I also brought this." Oscar handed Blake a camera. "We'll attach the infrared thermal camera to the drone. We'll be able to see exactly how many men are in and around Pablo's compound before we go in. This will give us an advantage."

An advantage they disparately needed. He looked at the drone and then to his friend. "This is great. Thank you."

"I have a few more things. Oscar turned and grabbed a duffel bag on the floor with both hands and passed it to Blake. "Police uniforms to help you blend in the event we are stopped on the way." There was a slight pause. "As well as the vests you requested."

Hal smiled and patted Oscar on the back. "This will really help. You're a good man."

"I've got a few quick calls to make and then let's get this show on the road. It's going to be a long drive." Blake glanced at this watch. "It'll be about three in the morning by the time we reach the compound. Sanchez and his men will be sleeping. The sooner we can get there, the sooner we get Whitney back."

Sixteen hours after they'd left the house in Tumaco, Blake fidgeted in the passenger seat. At one o'clock in the morning, anticipation chomped at his veins. He needed to find Whitey and get the hell out of this country. He tried to shake off the wave of worry that had been intensifying the closer they got to Sanchez's compound.

As Oscar sped down the desolate road toward Bogotá,

Mike and Hal sat in the back seat chatting.

"I still can't believe I'm sitting in a Renault," Mike said.

Hal laughed. "Do you still have that '69 cherry red Camaro?"

"Yeah. I can't seem to part with her. She's gotten us out of some tough jams over the years. Quite a few actually."

"This older make of vehicle is popular here, especially for the mountain terrain, and helps us blend in. I'd love to ride in your classic car one day," Oscar said.

Mike pat Oscar on the shoulder. "Anytime, my friend."

Blake stretched his legs and inhaled a deep breath then let it out. Before they'd left Tumaco he'd spoken to Trent Chambers and was happy to learn Jerry Maxwell had been released from the hospital. He'd make a full recovery. The guy had gotten off lucky. Like everyone else, the cameraman wasn't too happy about his new digs at the safe house with Blake's parents, Michelle, and Angel but it was the best place for him until this was all over.

And it was going to be over soon.

As they continued the drive time ticked by. Blake prayed Whitney was alive. The closer they got to Bogotá, the air turned crisp due to the high altitude and the road transformed into a pothole maze.

Oscar swerved the car around a large pothole the size of a small crater then slowed the car to a crawl. "There's a military check ahead."

"Shit," Mike said.

Blake sat up straight in the seat. Thankfully, Oscar had gotten them National Police uniforms to wear so they wouldn't stick out.

Two armed men in two-tone camo gear stood on either side of a security barrier setup in the middle of the road.

The danger factor just quadrupled.

"You sure they're soldiers?" Hal asked.

"They could be. They might be protecting Sanchez. Or a cocaine laboratory hidden in the jungle." Oscar glanced at Blake. "I'll do all the talking. Stay cool." He looked down at the passports next to him then quickly tucked them between the seat and out of sight. "Even though things have changed a lot in Colombia over the past twenty years the country is still very dangerous no matter where you go. Nothing is as it seems especially at night. Tourists are surprised to discover that we still have security guards walking around in our shopping centers carrying shotguns. Just because these guys look like military men doesn't mean we're safe. They could be on Pablo's payroll."

Blake had a bad feeling. This wasn't good. His face was on those wanted posters and the back of the Renault was loaded with weapons, ammunition, grenades, and a drone. If the car was searched...

He glanced over his shoulder at Mike and Hal.

Mike nodded. Clearly, he was getting the same vibe Blake was experiencing.

Blake's fingers itched for his gun under the seat. Something didn't feel right. He hoped he was wrong.

One of the camo-clad guys walked toward the car with his hand up in the air and ordered them to halt.

Oscar pressed his foot down on the brake and rolled to a stop. He lowered his window when the man approached.

A blast of cold air drifted through the car. The chill did nothing to stop the hair on the back of Blake's neck from standing at attention.

The military man flicked on a flashlight and shone it

inside the car then in each of their faces.

Tension filled the air.

Oscar held up his police credentials. "Capitán Oscar Moreno. Qué está pasando?"

Camo guy's eyes narrowed. "Lo sentimos, capitán." He paused for a long moment. "Hemos recibido la orden de revisar cada vehículo para la cocaína."

Blake knew enough Spanish to understand they were ordered to check every vehicle for cocaine. But with his face everywhere, he kept a close eye on camo guy and carefully moved his hand to his side closer to his weapon. Just in case.

The man flicked off the flashlight. "Adelante, Capitán." Then he waved to his partner a few hundred yards away to move the barrier from the road allowing them to drive through.

Blake let out the breath he was holding. "Jesus. I thought for sure he was going to search the car."

"Hope we don't hit another one of those," Hal said.

Oscar rolled up his window. "We shouldn't. We're about forty-five minutes from an old dirt road leading to the site where one of the largest cocaine laboratories in this area was located until it was dismantled years ago. It overlooks the compound. The perfect spot to use for setup."

CHAPTER SIXTEEN

Whitney's knees shook as Cortez dragged her by the chain through the house and into a mammoth living room with floor-to-ceiling windows overlooking a swimming pool. The walls were painted chocolate brown with glossy white trim that matched the finish on the coffee tables. She was surprised by the quality of the decor. Surprised by the cleanliness for a man who had slaughtered innocent people for years. There was even a black baby grand piano in the corner next to a dozen tropical plants. Alejandro ambled beside her with a permanent smirk on his face. Another man he called Eduardo stayed a step behind him with his gun visible.

Pablo was sitting on a white leather sectional with two young brunettes on either side of him snorting cocaine from a glass tray on the coffee table.

He lifted his head, sniffed, and wiped his nose with the back of his hand. "Our first guest has arrived." He snapped his fingers at the two women with movie star hair and makeup who might have been eighteen years old. "Go."

First? Blake wasn't here. She'd hoped he was here so they could escape together. Whitney's stomach did a dive and she swallowed the lump in her throat. Where was he?

The women climbed off the couch and giggled as they hastily left the room.

Pablo stood.

The top of his head almost touched the bottom of the crystal chandler hanging from the ceiling in the center of the room. His forehead glistened with sweat under the light, more than likely from the drugs he just did and not from the heat in the room. He unbuttoned his white shirt. A black and red serpent tattoo ran down his neck and stopped in the middle of his hairy chest.

Whitney cringed as he approached.

"Our friend Nathan Shaw was right. He told me a lot about you when we were in prison together. You are quite beautiful in person." He touched her hair rubbing the strands between his finger tips and looked over at her captor. "By the look of Cortez's face, quite deadly as well. But I already know how deadly you are, don't I, Whitney Steel? Two of my best men are dead because of you."

"Blake should have killed you when he had the chance three years ago at the Chevron station when you kidnapped Angel."

Pablo gritted his teeth, his eyes wide. He grabbed her by the throat. His big hand squeezed her neck.

Whitney gasped small breaths. She started to wheeze and choke as he pressed harder, cutting off her air supply.

She clawed at his hand. The metal cuffs and chain jangled.

He kept squeezing.

Her skin prickled and her lungs ached from the lack of oxygen. She tried to lift her leg to kick him in the stomach but lights flashed behind her eyes. Her vision blurred then doubled.

She was going to pass out.

"Enough." Alejandro put his hand on Pablo's arm. "Remember why you've kept her alive this long—for Blake Barnett to watch her die before you slit his throat. Remember Manuel."

Pablo released his grip then spun and let out an earth-shattering howl like a wild dog.

Whitney staggered back a few steps. She bent and gulped air until she caught her breath. Uncontrollable tears rolled down her checks. Once her breathing returned to normal she straightened and stared at the man who just tried to strangle her. "Go to hell. When Blake gets here he's going to kill all of you."

Pablo laughed. The high-pitched sound echoed throughout the room and made Whitney's skin erupt in goosebumps.

He sat back down on the couch and folded this arms across his chest. He looked at her captor. "Take her outside to meet Kato. Afterward, Eduardo will show you which room she will be in until her beloved Blake arrives."

Cortez nodded then pulled on the chain, her cue to get moving.

She dug the heels of her canvas shoes into the carpet to stop him and narrowed her eyes at Pablo. "He is coming for you." Whitney hoped to God Blake really was.

Pablo waved his hand. "Get her out of here."

Her captor led her out of the room while Eduardo followed. They headed down a long pathway past the pool. Dozens of underwater lights illuminated the deep sparkling water and lit their way as they walked through the expansive yard.

Something growled.

Whitney's heart stopped. So did her feet.

The low vibrating rumble was much louder—closer. She didn't like what she was hearing. It's sounded like a wild animal. Cortez forced her to keep walking. On the right, she spotted a large fenced enclosure with a laddered platform and metal chute like a curved slide at the far end.

Another growl.

Whitney squinted then her eyes widened.

A tiger stalked back and forth behind the fence.

Cortez glanced at her and grinned. "Meet Kato. Such a beautiful creature and quite deadly too."

Fear licked at Whitney's soul. Her pulse sped up. Now she knew what she'd heard when she'd first arrived.

The tiger stopped and turned into the light and looked at her.

Oh, God! The animal had a human skull with clumps of dark hair on it dangling out of its mouth. The sight made her gag. Bile rose in her throat. She inhaled through her nose and exhaled through her mouth to stop from throwing up.

"Move. Pablo wants you secure in a room." He nodded to Eduardo then back to her. "Don't worry, you won't be in there long. You are going to pay for Raul and Enzo."

Hurt or be hurt. Live or die.

Whitney wanted to live. She had to do something.

As the two men made her walk up to the house, a snapshot of the tiger lingered in her mind and so did the taste of fear. She remembered stories about how exotic animals were the "in thing" for drug lords—a show of wealth and prestige. She would never have believed it if she hadn't seen it with her own eyes. After seeing what she had, Whitney wondered if there were other animals on the property.

Things weren't going to end well for her. Blake had better show up soon. If he didn't, Whitney would be dead.

❊ ❊ ❊

While Mike and Hal unloaded the drone and other equipment from the back of the Renault, Blake, and Oscar stood in the clearing on the edge of the ravine. Below, Pablo's compound was well lit and on high alert, knowing Blake would be coming. The canopy was thick overhead and blocked out the glow of the full moon. From this height, the mansion was situated at the bottom of a huge bowl with mountains on each side. Beyond that, Bogotá slept. Its skyline of towering concrete and glass was laid out across flat land deep within the valley.

Blake peered through the night vision binoculars. "Doesn't look too sleepy in Pablo Town. There are two men out by the swimming pool. Three—no—four at the back of the house. But I don't see Whitney."

"Sanchez will keep her hidden. He wants you to come to him. He's counting on it."

Oscar was right. And Blake was counting on killing Sanchez and bringing Whitney home.

"We'll know soon enough." Blake looked to the west and spotted a big striped cat laying under a tree in a fenced-in area. "Christ, the bastard has a tiger."

"Over the years, I've heard stories but I didn't know if they were true. We need to make sure there aren't any other animals. The last we want to do is run into a wild cat. We'll know better once the drone is up in about ten minutes."

Mike and Hal walked up behind him carrying the drone, camera, remote control, receiver, and flashlights.

Mike set the drone on the ground and turned on one of the flashlights, giving them just enough light to work.

A cloud of tiny flies swarmed around him. Blake lowered the binoculars and looked at Hal and Mike. "In case you didn't hear. We might have a problem. Sanchez has a tiger. Be aware. There might be others on location."

"Why doesn't that surprise me?" Hal shook his head.

"Not really what you signed up for, is it, Hal?" Mike laughed and slapped him on the back.

"Not really. But that's okay. I brought some pretty big guns. Believe me—the guns will win."

Oscar got down on his knees and attached the infrared thermal camera to the mount underneath the belly of the drone then checked the propellers.

It was clear that Hal loved techie-type toys. He looked like a kid at Christmas, wide-eyed and a huge grin on his face. When this was over, Blake would make sure the guy got one.

Blake watched as Oscar tightened the landing gear. The thing looked like a mini spacecraft on landing skids. "I've never seen one of these up close and personal."

"Wait until you see what it transmits. It's actually quite stunning." Oscar turned on the unit and stood.

A red light flicked on and the motor fired up followed by a green indicator light.

Mike rubbed his chin and stepped back. "Cool."

"Perfect. The green light shows we've got a nice steady GPS signal from at least six satellites. We have to always have at least six." Oscar grabbed the remote control and receiver.

A loud crack.

A branch snapped to the right of them.

Mike, Hal, and Blake spun and drew their weapons at

the same time.

Blake aimed his gun high and scanned the wilderness around them. "See anything?" He kept his voice low, slightly above a whisper.

"Might be an animal." Oscar cautiously walked a few steps then stopped.

"Or militants," Hal added.

Blake hoped like hell it wasn't a giant cat like the one he just saw at Pablo's compound. He was also aware of the deadly havoc militants could play operating across a large swathe of jungle in pockets of rebel-held territories throughout Colombia.

A branch creaked followed by a reverberating flutter of leaves. Birds flew in all directions.

Mike bent for the flashlight and shone it up into the trees and had his gun pointed in the direction of the sounds.

Four monkeys with neon red faces and mangy fur jumped from tree to tree.

One turned its head and glared at Blake. "God damn monkeys. Just about gave me a stroke." He lowered his weapon. "Let's get back to work."

A few minutes later, Oscar manned the drone and it lifted off the ground. Small clear LED lights glowed on the bottom of the unit as it hovered and then flew, scouring above the trees and down the mountain toward Pablo's house.

The men huddled around Oscar and watched the images burst to life on the receiver.

Heat signatures popped up on the screen. Red, orange, and yellow images turned into human shapes one after another.

"There has to be at least twenty scattered in the jungle

outside the compound."

"Not going to be easy." Blake turned to Hal. "Once we know how many are inside, snipe as many as you can. We'll have to take out what's left on the way down."

"I'll get setup." Hal went to the car and got the sniper rifle out of the back.

The drone continued northward and flew over the house. Oscar kept it hovering over the roof long enough to get a good snapshot of what was going on.

Blake studied the screen. "I'm thinking Whitney might be right here." He pointed to the end of the house showing colorful outlines of two people outside a room —probably guards. "Everyone else seems to be gathered at the front of the house and the rest outside."

Mike glanced at Blake and shook his head in agreement. "It would make sense to keep her isolated. I can't wait to nail the bastard."

Neither could Blake. "So we've got about thirty plus the tiger. Hope we don't have to deal with that thing." Sweat broke out across his hairline even though the air was cool and damp.

Hal placed the M21 semi-automatic sniper rifle with a sound suppressor on the tripod rifle rest then lay on his belly.

"We've got about forty minutes before the drone is out of juice. We're going to have to be quick."

"I'm ready to go. Just say the word."

"Mike, get our bags from the car. The second Hal starts shooting I want to be ready to go downhill."

"You got it."

Five minutes later, Blake and Mike slipped the straps of the knapsacks over their shoulders and positioned them on their backs. Blake adjusted his vest then checked his weapon.

Mike set Oscar and Hal's knapsacks on the ground beside them, readied for when they were ready to descend down the mountain to the compound.

While Oscar flew the drone he recited coordinates.

Hal aligned the scope and placed the cross hairs on the first target. A few seconds passed. He fired.

The muzzle flashed. A bullet screamed through the night.

"Target down."

One by one, Blake watched the heat signatures vanish from the screen as Hal shot each of Pablo's men, clearing the way for them to make their move.

Hal grunted and climbed to his feet. "All clean kills." He quickly folded the tripod and rest and shoved them into his knapsack. After closing the bag, he put his knapsack on one shoulder and swung the rifle sling made of a rope tied to the barrel attached to the butt of the stock over his other.

Oscar handed the receiver and remote to Blake while he gathered his sack. "You ready?"

Blake drew a long deep breath and wiped the moisture that broke out over his upper lip. "I think so. Keep the drone ahead of us in case anything pops up. So far it looks like we haven't been discovered. Let's keep it that way."

As they made their way over the ravine and hiked cautiously through the winding foothills, bright stars and the full moon's glow lit the way. Oscar walked beside him piloting the drone and keeping an eye on the receiver's screen to ensure they hadn't been detected. Mike and Hal walked six feet ahead.

Hal held up his hand, signaling everyone to stop.

Blake felt the hairs on the back of his neck rise. "What

is it?"

"A tripwire. It runs over there." Hal pointed to a cluster of three trees about two feet away from where he and Mike were standing.

The area was booby trapped.

Blake knew Sanchez wouldn't make it easy. He didn't expect anything less from the cold-blooded killer. "Take it slow and keep your eyes open."

After they stepped over the tripwire, the men continued down the embankment for another twenty minutes. With each step, Blake scanned the jungle floor for anymore tripwires or hidden traps. His pulse pounded at his temples and he swore he'd swallowed at least a dozen small insects so far. The last one had lodged in his throat and made him cough. The sound of his dry hack echoed in the light breeze. Dozens of birds scattered and flew west into the tree tops.

Mike pointed to the left.

White smoke curled high above the leafy canopy.

"A cocaine lab." Oscar shook his head. "They never learn. They're a lot harder to hide at night, especially now with the use of drones and infrared cameras. The smoke would also be a dead giveaway during the day. Our helicopters search this area on a regular basis. We dismantle one—three new ones pop up. Wait. There's movement inside the house."

Blake glanced quickly at the screen. Two hot pink and yellow images moved inside then disappeared.

"The signal dropped. We lost three satellites. I have to bring it down." Oscar stopped and guided the drone back toward them. The white LED lights beamed above and hovered. He moved the remote-control stick and the unit slowly lowered to the ground and landed right in front of Blake. Oscar shut off the motor and packed the drone in his knapsack.

An adrenaline rush of anticipation ripped through Blake's body the closer they got to the house. He was going to bring Whitney home. He couldn't wait to see her—to hold her. That bastard had better not have hurt her otherwise Blake would make sure Pablo suffered long and hard before he killed him.

Something rustled beside him. He kept walking and peered out of the corner of his eye. A dark colored snake slithered through a bed of leaves and popped up its head before curling around a large rock. The thing had to be at least six feet long. He didn't know if it was venomous or not but he wasn't sticking around to find out. He picked up his pace and kept an eye out for anymore traps.

Oscar pat him on the back and smiled. "It's a ground snake. There's lots of those around here."

"Great."

An explosion rocked the jungle floor. The force of the blast almost knocked Blake off his feet. "What the hell?"

Orange flames raced up two trees behind them, sizzled and stripped the leaves from the branches.

Oscar peered at the burning trees and then to Blake. "I think the coke lab blew up. We need to get out of here."

Hal and Mike walked a few more feet then slowed. Hal threw up his hand then crouched next to a tree trunk.

Mike squatted beside him while Oscar kept his head low, and moved up next to them.

Headlights bounced back and forth. Two double-seated ATVs with two men on each bore down on them. Blake spun and ducked behind an enormous bush. He heard excited voices speaking in Spanish. The acrid smoky air mixed with the smell of gasoline as the vehicles raced by and drove in the direction of the explosion.

"This might be our chance." Oscar rubbed his right eye. "There's only one guard at the back of the house."

Blake glanced behind him. Flames raced up a coconut tree with a whoosh. Taillights on the ATVs faded and then disappeared into the brush. "Take him out."

Hal positioned the rifle and aimed.

Seconds later, the man at the back of the house dropped to the ground and slumped against the wall.

Afterward, they tore out of the jungle and scrambled down a stiff descent that opened into a patch of tall grass. Mud squished beneath their feet.

Blake thanked the universe for getting them out of the jungle without hitting a tripwire. He glanced sideways at the enclosed pen across from them and pointed to the tiger pacing inside the perimeter of the fence.

The beast let out a roar.

"Hope the noise doesn't attract any unwanted attention," Hal said as he stared at the wild animal.

Blake prayed it wouldn't too. They were too damn close to rescuing Whitney.

"Hal and Oscar. I want you guys to wait for the four on the ATVs to come back—take them out as soon and as quietly as possible." He'd counted six men originally which meant he didn't know where the last man had disappeared to. Blake assumed he'd gone inside the house. "Mike and I are going in."

"Good luck."

Oscar's voice was colored with concern. He wasn't the only one. Hal had a glint of worry in his eyes. Blake refocused on the tiger scratching its front paw along the dirt. "If that thing gets loose, shoot it." He didn't like being so close to a wild animal that could rip them apart. He thought about everything that could go wrong— the possibilities were endless. He scrunched down then threw off the knapsack and undid the flap. Blake grasped two M84 stun grenades and put one in each of his uniform shirt pockets as well as additional ammunition.

Mike screwed the silencer into place on the end of the 9mm Beretta pistol then shoved extra magazines into every empty pocket he had available. "Let's get this done."

❋ ❋ ❋

In the living room, Cortez downed a double shot of Aguardiente and thought about his wife. He prayed she had left the country with his sons like he'd asked her to do. Once he collected his money from Pablo for delivering the woman, he'd contact her. More than anything he looked forward to the day when he would be reunited with his family. Pablo couldn't discover the truth.

Alejandro passed him a cigar then lit one for himself. "Do you need a doctor to look at your face?"

His head hadn't stopped pounding since the woman had attacked him. "No, I'm fine. It looks much worse than it really is."

Pablo poured another glass of liquor then sat on the couch. "How did she kill them?"

Cortez knew his boss and Alejandro would want the details of Raul and Enzo's deaths. He should have just shot her when he had the chance. Instead, he was forced to dump his two friends in the desert. "The woman was very resourceful. She stabbed Raul in the neck with a metal fingernail file she had in her purse. Punctured an artery or something and he bled out."

Alejandro blew a puff of smoke toward the ceiling. The smoke bellowed and coiled around the chandelier. His eyes narrowed. "What about Enzo? What happened to him?"

"She used karate and kicked him, right here." He pointed at Alejandro's throat. "I've never seen a woman so skilled in martial arts before."

"Both died quickly?"

Raul had suffered but Cortez wasn't going to tell the older man. It wasn't something Alejandro needed to know. "Yes. Neither suffered." He lit his cigar and took a long drag. "I'm sorry I couldn't stop her. Everything happened so fast. She is much deadlier than your friend Nathan Shaw told you."

The muscles in Pablo's forearms jerked. "That whore will pay in more ways than one once Barnett shows up." He jumped off the couch and hurried to the windows. "Have Eduardo and the others returned from the lab explosion?"

"No. Not yet." Alejandro got out of the chair and stood behind Pablo.

Pablo snubbed his cigarette in the ashtray. "The man who killed my brother is finally here. Get everyone ready. It's time to kill Blake Barnett."

CHAPTER SEVENTEEN

At the back of the house, the dead man lay sprawled out on a stone pathway with a bullet hole through his heart. Clean kill was right. Blake and Mike grabbed the man's feet and dragged him into the shadows out of sight.

In the distance, Blake heard the engines before he spotted the ATV headlights ripping through the jungle and speeding to the tiger pen. "They're coming. Hal and Oscar need to take them out before they reach the house."

"We've got more company." Mike motioned to the other side of the house with his weapon.

Lights approached from the driveway.

They were stuck in the middle.

A car door slammed shut.

Heavy footsteps.

Blake flattened his back against the brick wall and held his breath.

A man hurried around the corner with his head down, fiddling with his cell phone.

Mike raised his gun and fired.

Swift. Silent. Deadly.

The man didn't know what hit him—didn't even know they were there other than he might have heard the pop of the silencer. The bullet cut into his forehead and exited out the back of his skull. He stiffened and toppled backwards on the lawn like a freshly cut tree.

Blake let out the breath he was holding. His eyes scanned the area in case there were more men lurking in the shadows. He didn't see anyone. "That must have been our missing man."

Mike nodded then peeked around the corner at the driveway. "All clear."

The high-pitched whine of an engine like a foot was stuck on a gas pedal and brake at the same time sounded.

The ATV bolted toward them with a man still sitting on it. It flew into a garden and clipped the corner of a rock.

Oscar and Hal were running behind it.

The machine spun in a half-circle and almost flipped over on its roll-bar before it landed in the swimming pool with a huge splash. Seconds later the vehicle sunk to the bottom of the pool.

If Pablo didn't know they were here, he would now.

"Shit. What the hell happened?"

Oscar was breathing hard, his face wet with sweat from running. "The others are dead. That one spotted us."

Hal bent over gasping for a breath with his one hand on his knee. "When I shot him, his damn hand froze on the accelerator. There was nothing we could do but chase him and shoot."

"What's the plan now?" Mike asked.

Blake was silent for a moment. He looked at Oscar. "You and Hal take the front of the house." He dug a stun grenade out of his shirt pocket and handed it to Oscar.

"Once you hear our grenade go off, toss yours. We know there's at least four to five men still inside—maybe more. And Whitney."

Mike rifled through the dead man's pockets and retrieved a set of car keys and held them in the air. "We've got a ride."

Blake felt better knowing they'd be able to get back to Oscar's safe house and work on their exit strategy to leave the country. It sure beat hiking through the jungle again with tripwires, snakes, and God knows what else. "They know we're coming so we've only got one shot at this. Get her and get out." His heart pounded against his chest wall. This was it. They were going to finally get Whitney.

After Hal switched out his sniper rifle for a hand gun, he and Oscar dashed down the driveway toward the front of the house.

Blake and Mike crept along the house snug to the wall and through the garden until they were next to a set of wide ground to ceiling windows. Light spilled from inside and shone across the lawn, casting eerie tall shadows on the water of the pool.

Blake squatted and peeked through the corner of the window. He didn't see anyone. "Ready?"

"Yeah."

While Mike picked up a large rock from the garden then stepped back a few feet, Blake reached into his pocket and grabbed the single detonation flash bang.

Mike threw the rock at the bottom of one of the tall windows. It hit the pane of glass with a loud crack. Shards of glass shattered and showered down to the ground. They now had their entry point.

Blake pulled the pin on the grenade, careful to keep

pressure on the safety lever. He hurled the cylinder as far as he could inside and sprinted away from the house as he covered his ears. Mike tore around the corner to the driveway.

Intense heat, a split-second quick flash of over a million candlepower of light, and one hundred and eighty decibels of ear splitting bang rocked the mansion.

Glass broke at the front of the house.

Men yelled.

Another blinding flash and deafening bang. Then a puff of gray smoke.

Mike and Blake hurtled through the opening where the window once was with their guns drawn. The smell of burnt mercury and magnesium powder filled the air. A man in the corner of the room had his hands over his ears disoriented, stumbling into the furniture. Blake couldn't see his face but spotted the weapon in the man's hand.

Mike fired.

The bullet tore into the man's chest. He screamed and jerked around like a marionette then slumped to the floor like a ragdoll. Blake looked at the dead man's face. He swore under his breath. The guy wasn't Pablo or Cortez. The two men he only cared about.

Inching down the hall, Blake stayed low and entered the kitchen while Mike checked the dining room. Moments later, Mike gave the 'all clear' signal then pointed to the hallway. Blake nodded.

Shots rang out.

Blake ducked behind the island in the kitchen and groped his gun. More rounds followed by the rat-a-tat of an assault rifle. Wood splintered above him. Plates and glasses shattered into a million pieces and hailed down around him. Blake covered his head with his arm to protect himself from the flying debris. A bullet whistled by him and thumped into the front of the dishwasher with a clink. He cringed. He ejected the magazine and slapped another one in place.

Then the gunfire suddenly stopped.

Minutes passed and Blake peeked around the island.

He didn't see anyone.

Where the hell was Pablo?

He drew a deep breath and ran to the far end of the kitchen, his knapsack flapping against his back. He spotted Mike crouched in the bathroom. Hal had his back to the wall of the staircase with his gun aimed at the top of the stairs. From Blake's angle, he couldn't see Oscar.

He raced across the hall to the washroom where Mike was now standing. "Where are they?"

Mike shrugged. "Up or down. They scattered when Hal started shooting."

He shook off the knapsack and let it slide to the floor. Blake quickly filled his pockets with more magazines. "We've got to hurry. The sun's coming up. You and Oscar take the garage. Have Hal go downstairs. I'm going up. I have a feeling that's where Pablo is keeping her."

"Be careful, man. We'll meet out front. I'll make sure our vehicle is ready to roll."

Blake patted him on the shoulder. "Keep your eyes open. I want everyone to get out of this alive."

After the guys disappeared out of sight, Blake gripped his gun with two hands and climbed the first five steps. Something moved, like light footsteps. He stopped and glanced over his shoulder, unsure where the sound was coming from, then looked back to the top of the stairs. He took careful steps up the rest of the stairs. The hallway seemed to stretch forever and was empty.

Gunfire erupted below him on the lower floor. Hal had run into someone and Blake hoped it was Sanchez. He also hoped that Hal had already put a slug in the bastard's head saving him the trouble.

The house turned abruptly quiet.

When his foot touched the landing, one of Pablo's men tore out of a room with an assault rifle at his side and skidded to a stop.

Blake aimed at the man's forehead. "Where's the woman?" His mind registered that Whitney might already be dead. He shook away the thought and focused on what was standing in front of him.

The guy stared at him, his eyes narrow slits. "No lo sé."

From his tone and the expression on his face, Blake knew he was lying. He knows.

His hand twitched on the rifle.

Blake squeezed the trigger. The man dropped to the floor in a tangled heap.

He stepped over him, his fingers curled tightly around the grip of his gun, and swept the long hallway, left to right, room by room. So far he'd come up empty. His pulse pounded in his neck and his jaw tightened. He had to find Whitney. He couldn't give up. He wasn't going home without her.

Blake checked the next doorknob and turned it slowly. The door clicked open and he peered inside. Empty. He crept to the next room. This time the door was ajar. He placed his back against the wall and kept his weapon upright and ready to shoot if need be. No sign of Whitney.

Ten yards away, light spilled out across the ceramic floor from the bottom of a closed door. Hairs on his arms stood up. Something wasn't right. He looked over his shoulder. The house was too quiet. Where were the guys? It had been at least ten minutes since the last gun shot. He had to remain focused on finding her.

Hunched over with his gun, Blake searched the next two rooms. Both empty. At the third door, he looked down. Shadows flittered in and out, stretching in the light under the door. Someone was inside. Whitney? Pablo? He reached and slowly turned the door knob. It was locked. His head snapped to the dead guy on the floor. Dark red blood pooled around the man's head and ran along the side of his body.

Blake hurried down the hall and rummaged through the guy's pockets for a key. God damn it. Nothing. He'd have to take his chances and kick in the door—no telling what was on the other side. Back at the room, he stood across from the door. After drawing a deep breath, Blake twisted and lifted his right foot and kicked the center of the door. Dust puffed out from the frame.

No gun shots from the other side. A good sign but he still wasn't sure what he was walking into on the other side.

He grunted and nailed it with the heel of his hiking boot. The wood buckled and rattled, then fell off one of its hinges. With one last kick, the door burst open.

✽ ✽ ✽

Whitney had locked herself in the bathroom and scrunched down in the shower stall. She'd heard glass shattering, deafening bangs, and a lot of gun shots earlier. Then it became quiet except for a single shot coming from the hallway.

For over two hours she had paced the bedroom trying to figure out a way to escape. There was no way out. She'd checked the two windows and yanked on the steel bars for what seemed like an eternity but they wouldn't budge. Pablo had made damn sure she couldn't leave. When she couldn't find a way out, Whitney needed something to hang on to so she sat in the bathroom away from the noise and thought about Blake and when they'd first met at ShawBioGen. He'd been working undercover, using a fake name, searching for proof that Nathan was responsible for his sister Claire's death. Whitney closed her eyes. Back then she had thought he was an arrogant jerk. Boy, was she wrong. No matter what happened next in this house, she loved him with all her heart.

"Welcome to ShawBioGen, Miss Steel. I'm Blake Neely, the company's security specialist."

Whitney gave him a quick once-over. Dressed in black jeans, cowboy boots, and an open-necked shirt with its sleeves rolled back over his forearms, he was tanned and well-toned.

"Isn't a security specialist just a fancy title for a body-guard?"

Lines crept across his forehead. "You need to sign in," he said in a firm even tone as he shoved a clipboard and pen at her.

After signing her name, she noticed an x-ray machine at the end of the long counter. If security were this tight here, she'd have no hope in hell of getting into a lab where Nathan kept the child.

Next Blake slid a tray in front of her. "Empty your purse."

"You're kidding, right?"

With his arms crossed in front of his chest, Blake shook his head.

"And I thought airport security was tough." Whitney chuckled and dumped the contents of her purse onto the tray. While he picked through them, she wondered what kind of

man lurked behind those deep-set brown eyes.

"Sorry, no cameras. You can pick this up on the way out."

"Fine, but—" She reached toward him, but was a second too late. "Those are—"

He clicked open the gold and black leopard print case. Four foil-wrapped condom packages fell on the counter. Unsure if she should be angry or embarrassed, she felt her face flood with heat. To make matters worse, he took his sweet time inspecting each package, obviously getting her back for the bodyguard comment.

He raised an eyebrow. "Twisted Pleasure. Rough Rider. Must be for cowboys. And this one, Paradise..."

Their gazes collided.

Her body hummed with electricity so intense her heart raced and her breasts tingled. Raw lust.

She snatched the condoms out of his hand, upset he had this effect on her. "Do you mind? Aren't you getting a bit personal?"

"Personal or not, you'd be surprised at what these packages can be used for." He snatched them back, tossed them on the conveyor belt, and grinned. "Better safe than sorry."

The sound of wood splitting made Whitney's head snap to the bathroom door.

She stepped out of the whirlpool bathtub and quietly turned the lock. After cracking the door open just enough see most of the room she heard someone whisper, "Whitney."

For a second, she thought she was dreaming.

"Are you in here?"

The sound of Blake's voice made her knees weak. It really was him. The heavy weight on her chest lifted. She could breathe again. Her legs buckled, and she grabbed the marble counter to steady herself, so she wouldn't fall.

It was over.

He'd finally come for her.

She opened the door. Tears filled her eyes and fell on her cheeks.

He smiled then wrapped his arms around her and held her tight. "Honey, are you okay?"

Her heart melted. The warmth of his arms, the familiar smell of his body. For a moment, her voice was gone, and she couldn't talk. She just wanted to be held, to know this was real.

"I love you." He kissed her forehead and then released her.

She didn't want him to let go. But she knew they had to get out the house. "I'm okay." She ran her fingers through his hair. "Your hair."

"I know. It's a long story." He glanced toward the hallway. "We've got to find Mike, Hal, and Oscar."

"Oscar?"

He smiled again and her heart melted for a second time. All the stress of the last few days vanished from her muscles.

"Yeah. Another long story." He turned his back to her. "Here. Check the bag. There's another gun inside. I have a feeling you're going to need it."

She undid the flap and pulled out a Beretta. "M9A1. Accurate and deadly." All those years of weapons training growing up would come in handy for the second time in her life. She had her father to thank and countless hours on the firing range. "What about Pablo and Cortez?"

The muscles in his jaw twitched. "I haven't found either of them yet—unless the guys have."

She tried to control her hands from trembling but failed.

"It's okay." He grasped her hand and held it. "We'll find them."

"We can't leave until they're dead." The words she just blurted out made her pause for a long moment, not sure if Blake was aware she'd killed Raul and Enzo. "I killed two men." *I didn't have a choice.*

"I know. You had to. Don't think about it. You did what you had to do to survive." He wrapped an arm around her shoulder and kissed her temple. "Ready?"

She nodded and tightened her grip on the gun.

"Stay close. If you see Pablo or Cortez—shoot."

❊ ❊ ❊

Blake halted at the bottom of the steps leading to the great room on the lower floor. He grabbed Whitney's arm and pulled her behind him, determined to shield her. He aimed his weapon at Pablo.

Sanchez had his gun pointed at the side of Oscar's head while Cortez had a rifle directed at Mike and Hal. Another man with gray hair sat in a chair looking as if he was enjoying the scene. Blake had no idea who the man was, but he planned on permanently removing the smirk off the guy's face.

"The gang's all here." Pablo sniffed and ground his teeth. "What are you going to do now, Barnett? Who are you going to try to save?" He laughed and waved his gun at Oscar's head. "The cop? One of your friends? The woman?"

Blake remained silent out of fear that Sanchez would snap and kill Oscar. One thing was certain, the bastard wasn't getting another go at Whitney. He glanced at Cortez. The bruises told a story. By the injuries to his face, Whitney had given him one hell of a shit kicking.

He'd gotten off pretty lucky compared to his two friends. He noticed Mike was holding his arm. Blood ran down his shirt and dribbled onto the carpet. They had to get out of this otherwise they were dead.

"Mike, you okay?"

"Yeah. Just a graze."

"Shut the fuck up, both of you."

Blake's focus shifted to the space separating himself and Pablo, waiting for the slightest movement, a flick of an eye or a muscle twitching.

Pablo jerked the gun at Oscar. He sniffed twice and swiped his hand over his nose. He stared at Blake. "You killed my brother and your whore killed Raul and Enzo. Three dead. All family. So, I get to kill three of you."

The muscles under Blake's shirt tensed. He could tell Sanchez was jacked on coke by the way his brown eyes were glossy and bloodshot. Not a good sign. He'd shoot Oscar without so much as a blink.

"Let the others go, Sanchez. It's me you really want." He needed to draw Pablo's attention away from Oscar and to him.

Whitney stepped out from behind and stood beside him, her gun aimed at Pablo. "Blake—no. He'll kill you."

"Of course, I will. The same way he slit Manuel's throat. *Ojo por ojo.* An eye for an eye." He pulled out a knife from his back pocket.

Fury and hate swirled through Blake. If Sanchez killed him, he wouldn't see Whitney again. Blake wasn't going to allow her to be at the mercy of that bastard. Not happening. He had just gotten her back.

"Alejandro, which two do you think should pay for Raul and Enzo deaths?"

The gray-haired man rose slowly to his feet. "The

woman and him." He pointed to Mike.

Now he knew who the man was. Alejandro Quintero. Ex-Colombian National Army and Pablo's number one in charge of the cartel's US network. He didn't have much time. Blake caught Mike's attention and winked.

This had to end now.

Blake held up his hands. "Okay, you win, Sanchez. I am all yours." He slowly lowered his hands. "I'm putting my gun and bag down." He bent and set his weapon on the carpet then shimmied the knapsack off his back. His heart pounded. This had better work.

One of the shoulder straps slid down his arm and landed in his hand. With his head turned away from Sanchez, he looked up and mouthed to Whitney, *Be ready.* Her grip tightened on the gun.

Rage exploded inside him. Blake heaved the knapsack with as much force as he could then scooped his gun up from the floor.

The bag smacked Pablo in the gut and sent him catapulting backwards into an end table. His gun went off. A slug drove into the ceiling.

Blake let off a round. The bullet hit the wall behind Sanchez with a thud.

Whitney fired two shots.

Pablo dropped and rolled around a corner out of sight. "You're dead, Barnett!"

Hal punched Cortez in the head, knocking him off balance.

Bullets sprayed the room from the assault rifle, sending everyone for cover.

Mike dove next to a wall-long entertainment center.

Hal hit the ground and crawled behind the couch.

"Come on!" Blake grabbed Whitney's hand and raced

up the stairs into the kitchen behind the island. "Stay here. I'm going to finish this."

"Be careful."

Oscar moaned as he limped into the kitchen, his face white as a bleached sheet. Blood pumped and soaked his left thigh and down his pant leg, dripping on the floor. "Alejandro—in the garage."

"Shit." Blake stared at the amount of blood Oscar was losing. He'd bleed out if they didn't do something quick. He put his arm around his friend's shoulder and eased him down, leaning him against the fridge. He saw the fear in the man's eyes. "You're going to be fine." He unbuckled his belt and ripped it off. "Whitney. Here. Use this as a tourniquet. Keep an eye on the color of his leg. If it doesn't look right, remove it and apply pressure."

She nodded. Her hands trembled.

"You can do this." Blake bent and kissed her cheek. "I'll be right back."

An engine roared.

"God damn it." *They can't get away.* He scrambled through the kitchen and thumped down the stairs. He stopped on the last step. "Mike. Hal. You guys okay?"

"I'm fine," Mike said.

"Me too. I'm going to kill that son of a bitch."

Blake was relieved to hear their voices. They were okay but worry chewed at his gut. Oscar was bleeding to death upstairs and he didn't know where Cortez went.

"Mike, where's Cortez?"

"I saw him go out through the garage with Alejandro."

Shit. Now, Blake, had two other lunatics running free to worry about. "Put down your weapon and come out. It's over, Sanchez."

Pablo laughed. "It's not over. Not until I kill you. The

war has just begun, Barnett. Do you think that if you kill me it will stop anything?" He laughed again. "There are thousands on the cartel's payroll. You won't be safe anywhere in your precious United States."

"You're outnumbered. All your other men are dead. Alejandro and Cortez are next."

"They've gone for backup. In a few minutes, the house will be swarming with my men—men who will do anything for a million dollar bounty. There's a price on your head, remember?"

That meant they didn't have long. Blake cursed under his breath.

Whitney screamed.

Blake tore up the stairs two at a time and slid to a stop in a puddle of blood on the kitchen floor. He raised his gun with two hands and aimed at the man's forehead.

Cortez pressed the knife against her throat. "Put the weapon down. Now."

Whitney's eyes were wide with fear. A thin red stream snaked down her neck.

Blake gritted his teeth. He was cutting her. He wasn't hurting her again.

Oscar somehow found the strength to kick Cortez in the leg and forced him to look down. He lowered the knife enough for Whitney to drop to the floor.

Blake squeezed the trigger.

Cortez's head flew back and slammed into the cupboard then forward. He was dead the second Blake had fired the gun. He helped Whitney up. "Are you okay?"

"Yes. But—"

"Speed dial two." Oscar held out a cell phone. His hand shook uncontrollably. "Call Juan. He knows what to do. Tell him—get my wife and daughter to the safe house.

Bring medical supplies." His arm went limp.

Blake grasped the phone and made the call. Afterward, he set the phone on the counter.

"He's unconscious. We need to get him help."

"I know." His friend was dying. Blake couldn't allow that to happen. He ejected the clip from the gun and inserted a fresh one then grabbed the knife. "Take care of him."

With each step, anger boiled and fueled his need to kill Pablo. He stomped down the steps with purpose—to finally end this nightmare. At the second last step, he threw the knife across the room. It stuck in the wall behind where Sanchez was hiding.

The abrupt movement forced Pablo to skitter away from the wall and out enough for Blake to get a clear shot.

In slow motion, he turned his head and looked at Blake. He smiled and raised the barrel of his gun.

"Go straight to hell." The gun barked as Blake fired three times.

The first shot hit Sanchez in the chest. The second in the stomach. The third bullet struck him in the right eye and left a gaping hole clear through the back of his head.

Blake stood there for a long moment, his legs shaking, transfixed on the bloody scene in the corner of the room.

It was over.

Pablo Sanchez was dead.

Then he saw Mike and Hal. "We need to get Oscar to the safe house or he isn't going to make it."

CHAPTER EIGHTEEN

B lake knew there was a good chance they would lose Oscar if they couldn't control the bleeding.

While Hal steered the Range Rover they'd taken from Pablo's house down the tortuous mountain, Whitney applied pressure to Oscar's leg wound using a bunched up T-shirt.

Blake sat on one side of him, Whitney on the other. He was still unconscious, his breathing ragged and shallow. His skin was pasty white and slick with sweat in the mid-morning sunlight.

Mike turned in the passenger seat and passed Blake two bottles of water. "How's he doing?"

"Not good. His pulse is pretty weak." He grabbed the water and opened one for Whitney. "We've got to get to that safe house soon."

Blake touched her hand and noticed bluish-red bruises around both her wrists. He didn't know what she'd gone through after Cortez and his pals had kidnapped her. Whatever it was, she was strong and she'd find a way to deal with it. He wasn't going to push her. When she was ready to talk, she would. And he'd be there for her. "Why don't you take a break. I'll take over."

"There's a chance he might not make it, isn't there?"

There was sadness in her eyes when she spoke. She scrubbed her bloodstained hands on one of the disinfectant wipes they'd found at Pablo's house while he pressed the cloth down on Oscar's thigh. He checked the pulse in the man's neck. Weak and irregular.

"Oscar's strong as an ox. Things aren't looking good, though." Blake glanced out the window. *Come on, man. You've got to pull through.* "He's a good guy. A good cop."

"I didn't know he was a police officer."

"Yeah. We've known him for quite a few years. He saved Mike's life—and mine."

"I'm sorry. I hope he pulls through." She looked over her shoulder and out the back window.

He slipped his hand in hers and squeezed. Her fingers trembled. Not a good time to tell her about the wanted poster or what Pablo had said before Blake killed him. All he could do was try to reassure her and pray he was right. "It's going to be okay."

"I don't know. I really don't. Pablo might be dead but Alejandro escaped. He could come after us just like Pablo did." She looked away and then back to him. "He said something strange. I can't seem to shake it. He said, 'You're like your father. You look just like him.' He said it in the present tense as if my father is alive. Blake, my father died in nineteen ninety-seven on assignment here. I don't understand. What Alejandro said doesn't make sense."

No, it didn't make sense, but Blake had a feeling the man just wanted to get under her skin and judging by the worry lines furrowing across her forehead, he'd succeeded. "Probably just a slip of the tongue and nothing more. Try not to worry about Alejandro."

She was right. He could come after them. However,

they had a bigger problem right now—one he didn't want to discuss. Any of Sanchez's associates in the US could come after them. He'd have to figure out how he was going to keep everyone in his life safe. Blake didn't want to think about it. Not right now.

He changed the subject on purpose in hopes of making her feel better—and himself. "Hey, we're going home to get married and Angel can't wait. She misses you like crazy."

Whitney smiled. "I miss her too. I can't wait to see her."

"Me too, honey."

As they drove for the next two hours the surroundings on the desolate roadway became familiar. Blake estimated they were less than an hour away from the safe house. He checked Oscar's wound and replaced the blood-soaked T-shirt with a clean one then continued to apply pressure. His friend didn't look any better or worse. The bleeding seemed to have slowed somewhat.

Whitney's head rested against the window. Her eyes were closed. She was sound asleep.

He spotted red marks around her neck forming the faint outline of a hand and fingers. Blake's muscles tensed. He leaned his head back on the seat and forced back the anger brewing inside him. He was glad he killed Sanchez and Cortez. No regrets. No one would ever hurt her again.

Hal pointed out the window. "Those are coffee plants. What I wouldn't give for a cup of java right now."

In the rugged mountain terrain, Blake spotted Christmas-tree-like plants with dark green leaves and cherry red fruit. "I'd kill for a nice hot extra-large."

Mike peered around the seat. "Yeah, me too. It's been a

long few days."

"How's your arm?"

"It's okay. I'll survive. How's Oscar doing?"

"About the same. Hopefully, his wife will be able to help him."

Forty-five minutes later, Hal steered into the driveway and threw the Range Rover in park behind the house.

Blake touched Whitney's hand.

Her eyes flew open.

"It's okay. I didn't mean to scare you. We're here."

Relief flooded her face. Fine lines around her mouth and eyes relaxed.

Juan ran out of the house and met them. "How is he?"

Hal shook his head. "He's hanging on."

After Mike and Blake carried the wounded man inside the house, Oscar's wife, Mariana, pointed to the hallway. "Put him in the first bedroom. I brought supplies from the clinic. Everything is ready." She appeared calm and focused, determined to save her husband's life.

She was an attractive petite woman with a soft mouth and hard-working hands. Sofia stood beside her with her hand over her mouth at the sight of her father. The young woman looked more like her father, with the same twinkling brown eyes.

In the bedroom, they laid Oscar flat on his back on the mattress. An IV pole with a bag of clear liquid and a bag of blood attached to it was setup next to the bed. Mariana cut open Oscar's pant leg. Blood ran freely down the side of his leg. She snatched a stack of gauze. "Sofia. Press right here, on the femoral artery."

The young woman didn't hesitate. With her eyes glossed over with wetness, she sprang into action and held her hand firmly on the gauze. Mariana checked her husband's blood pressure. When she was done, she undid the cuff and removed the stethoscope from her ears. Her eyes met Blake's.

He spotted fear and sadness and something else—a sign that his friend might not make it. It was the look in her eyes combined with the stuttered sigh. Blake had a hollow pit in his stomach.

This wasn't going to end well.

Mariana quickly wiped Oscar's arm with antiseptic then inserted the IV catheter.

"What can we do to help?" Whitney asked.

Blake grasped her hand and held it.

"Someone bring the sterilized water from the kitchen. I'll need it to clean the wound."

"I'll get it," Hal said.

He returned a few minutes later and set the gallon jug of water on the nightstand. Mike stood in the corner of the room by the closet with the look of defeat on his face the way his eyebrows came together.

Mariana bent and kissed Oscar's forehead. She whispered something to him in Spanish then paused for a long moment before she spoke. "Could everyone leave us, please? I would like some time with my husband and daughter."

In the living room, Blake paced. Worry gnawed at his gut. Oscar had to make it.

Juan sat on the floor in the hallway outside of the bedroom.

Mike was at the desk on the laptop working on their exit plan while Whitney and Hal were in the kitchen making coffee and something for everyone to eat.

Food was the last thing Blake wanted. He couldn't stop thinking about Oscar. If he hadn't asked his friend to help them go after Pablo, he wouldn't be in the bedroom dying. His hands curled into fists and he wanted to punch something.

"Just got an email from Chambers. There's a privately contracted US aide flight coming in at Gerardo Tobar López Airport in Buenaventura at eleven tomorrow morning. The airport's about a fourteen hour drive from here. Our contact on the ground is ex-US military intelligence."

"Perfect." Blake checked his watch. Five after two. No matter what they couldn't miss the flight. It might be their only chance to leave the country.

"He said arrangements have already been made on the ground and to just get there."

Blake wasn't sure about what arrangements had been made. But he was grateful for any help. "Did you tell him about Oscar?"

Mike nodded. "He told me to tell you to bring Mariana and Sofia and—Oscar if he makes it. He said he'd figure it out and deal with the paperwork later."

Chambers had pulled through again. At this rate, Blake might actually start liking the guy. At least now they had a plan and Blake felt better knowing he had options for Oscar's family regardless of what happened to his friend. If Oscar died, he would make sure his family was safe. If they stayed in Colombia they would probably be killed by the cartel. With Sanchez, dead anything could happen, and Blake wasn't feeling very secure with Alejandro running free. He just didn't know how much power the man had in Colombia.

"Hey, Juan. Is there any place we can ditch the Range Rover? I'm not feeling too comfortable since it belonged to one of Pablo's men."

"I can get rid of it. My brother has a garage ten minutes from here. We can dump it there."

"Thanks. I'll have Mike or Hal go with you in a while."

Juan rose and shoved his hands in his pockets. "Is Pablo Sanchez dead?"

"Yes. I killed him."

Juan smiled and put his hand on Blake's arm. "Gracias." He made the sign of the cross against his chest. "Now my wife and son can rest in peace."

Whitney poked her head in the living room. "There's fresh coffee and sandwiches in the kitchen for anyone who wants them."

Her voice sounded small and fatigued. They still had a long journey ahead. Blake couldn't wait to be on their way home.

After everyone loaded their plates with lunch they sat in the living room and ate. Every now and then Blake thought he heard soft cries coming from the bedroom. He should never have asked Oscar to help them.

Mariana and Sofia came out of the bedroom holding hands. Their eyes were wet with tears.

Blake's heart skipped a beat. *No.* He dropped his half-eaten sandwich on his plate.

"Oscar is gone."

While Mike and Whitney tried to comfort Sofia in the living room, Hal and Juan went to dump the Range Rover. In one of the other bedrooms, Blake sat with Mariana. A heavy emptiness weighed on his chest. When he got back to Las Vegas he was going to knock Nathan Shaw off his God damn feet. The bastard wasn't going to get off scot-free. Not now with Oscar dead. The man was just as re-

228 | KIM CRESSWELL

sponsible for Oscar's death as Sanchez was. If he hadn't conspired to kidnap Whitney, Oscar would be alive. Nothing would give Blake more satisfaction than punching Shaw right between his beady little eyes.

"You're coming with us. You and Sofia will be much safer in the United States. You'll never be safe here. Once Alejandro learns that Sanchez is dead, he will come for you and your daughter. He will kill both of you."

Mariana cocked her head to one side and stared at him. "You know what Oscar told me? He said he wanted to help his American friends make a difference by ridding the country of a man who had terrorized the Colombian people for so many years. He was a hard-working man who loved his job as much as he loved his family. He died doing what he enjoyed doing—going after the bad guys, the chicos malos who murder women and children." She sniffed and wiped her nose with a tissue. "He'd be happy knowing Pablo Sanchez is dead. But I am not leaving my country. Not yet. I'm staying to bury my Oscar and afterward Juan will take me to my sister's home in Panama City."

"I wish you'd reconsider."

She shook her head. "No. There is nothing to reconsider. Please take Sofia. She's young. She's just starting her life. Panama City is no place for her. She's a good girl. She loved her father very much. Please protect her for Oscar. Not for me."

The woman was killing him. Blake swallowed the hard lump in his throat. He wasn't keen on leaving Mariana behind. As much as he didn't want to, he would abide by her decision. It was her life, not his. He was confident that Juan would make sure she got to her sister's house.

"I'll keep your daughter safe. You have my word."

"I believe you." She clasped his hands in hers. "Now I see what Oscar saw in you. You're a good friend, and a good man, Blake. I wish things had ended differently but we all knew the risks, especially Oscar. Thank you for trying to save my husband."

CHAPTER NINETEEN

At three in the morning, the moon peeked out from behind a litter of clouds and a cool breeze oscillated throughout the car. They had been driving for ten hours straight. Whitney stretched her cramped legs. She couldn't wait to be back home—back to normal. The first thing she wanted to do was shower and change her clothes. She'd been wearing the same jogging suit for days.

As Blake drove, Sofia slept in the backseat between Mike and Hal. The young woman's long dark hair fanned around her face like angel wings. Whitney's heart hurt for her—fatherless and now heading to a new country.

She wished Mariana had come with them but she understood the need to stay and bury her husband. Just like Whitney had buried her father. Alejandro's words still haunted her and left a nagging feeling she couldn't quite describe. More like an 'unfinished' feeling. *"You're like your father. You look just like him."*

What he said didn't make sense.

Her father was dead.

Whitney had buried him next to her mother.

She trampled the thought and turned her attention

to Blake. She was worried about him. Deep worry lines crinkled the corners of his eyes. He'd taken Oscar's death hard. They all had. He hadn't said much since they left the house.

Blake's jaw tightened. "I told Mariana I would protect Sofia. Are you okay with her coming to live with us?"

"Of course I am." She held his hand a little tighter. "I wouldn't expect anything less from you. Oscar was your friend. Friends help friends."

"And that's why I love you." He kissed her hand. "You're so easy to get along with. I can't wait to get you home."

Whitney smiled. "I can't wait to be home."

Hal laughed.

Blake looked over his shoulder then back to the road. "Man, I thought you were sleeping."

"Nope. Just resting my eyes. Mike's awake too." Blake slowed the vehicle. *God damn it.* "We've got a problem."

Whitney sat up straight in the seat and peered through the windshield. She shook her head. "This can't be happening. We're so close to getting out of the country."

A barricade. A generator. Lights.

Two jeeps, machine guns mounted on top, were parked on either side of the blockade with their motors running. Close to a dozen armed men stood in the middle of the road in front of the vehicles.

"They sure as hell aren't military. They're wearing balaclavas," Hal said.

Whitney turned in the seat and looked at Sofia. Her eyes were wide. She was terrified. "It's okay."

"Are they going to hurt us?"

"No. We won't allow that to happen. Just stay close to

Mike and do what he tells you. Everything will be fine."

Sofia nodded and shrunk back in the seat.

Mike passed a handful of ammunition to Blake. "They look like rebels. Marxist maybe."

He tossed a few magazines in his shirt pockets and placed the rest under the seat. He grabbed his gun and put it under his leg out of view.

Whitney slid the gun out and inserted a fresh magazine then put the weapon in her jogging suit pocket. Her hands shook. She was a reporter. Not a bloody commando. She was sick of fighting—sick of killing to survive. She just wanted to go home.

Blake rolled the car to a stop about fifty yards from the barricade. "How many do you see, Hal?"

Four men walked up the road. Two on each side of the car with their assault rifles pointed at the ground. One was carrying a piece of paper.

"I count eleven total including the two manning the guns on the jeeps. I've got two bangs ready. If they force us out of the car, I'll toss them at the jeeps. That will give us the best chance at taking the rest out if we have to."

Blake gave her hand a squeeze. "It's going to be okay."

Flashlight beams played against the vegetation. They were outnumbered.

Whitney's legs trembled. She couldn't imagine what Sofia was feeling. She had to be scared to death.

One of the men stopped at the driver's side window. He bent and looked inside the car. "Get out. Everyone."

Whitney was surprised the man spoke English. She slowly climbed out and kept her eye on the two rebels on her right and their guns. Mike and Sofia got out and stood behind her. Out of the corner of her eye, she spotted Hal next to Blake.

The man shoved a paper in Blake's face. "You look like the hombre in this picture. You're worth a million dollars."

"You've got the wrong guy. He's in Tumaco. We saw him. We just came from there."

The man lifted his gun and rammed the butt of it into Blake's stomach.

He doubled over and moaned.

Whitney had no idea what the man was talking about but she wasn't going to watch him hurt Blake. "Leave him alone."

One of the rebels beside her snatched her ponytail and dragged her back toward him. Moist breath touched the back of her neck.

Blake held up both his hands. "Okay. Okay. I'm the man in the picture. Let her go. Sorry but you're not going to get any money. Pablo Sanchez is dead. I killed him tonight."

The man laughed and so did the other three. "Sanchez isn't dead. You lie." He raised the butt of his gun again and struck Blake in the shoulder.

Whitney heard a crack. She winced.

"It's the truth. He's dead. We were all there. He's in his house up on the mountain with half his head gone," Hal said. He took a couple steps forward and off to the side.

She could tell he was positioning himself so he could throw the grenades. She snaked her hand into her pocket and grasped her gun. Her eyes met Hal's.

He gave a small nod.

Whitney shoved her heel into the man's kneecap behind her. There was a loud snap before he let go of her hair and tumbled backwards clutching his leg. He tried to get up but she kicked him in the chin knocking him unconscious.

Gunfire rattled back and forth.

Hal threw both grenades. Each hit their intended targets.

Mike shot the other rebel beside Whitney then put his arm around Sofia and shielded her as they ran and ducked behind a tree.

Two earth rattling bangs and an orange flash rocked the air followed by a puff of billowing white smoke.

Whitney seized the side of the car door to steady her feet. Her head felt fuzzy and hurt as if someone had hit her in the head with a cement brick. The pain was excruciating. Her ears rang so loudly all she could hear were muffled gun shots.

A silhouette barreled at her with a rifle pointed at her head. She stabilized her weapon with two hands. The bullet ripped into the man's shoulder and spun him sideways. Whitney fired again. This time the slug drilled into the back of his head and sent him plummeting away from her.

Shouts came from behind her but came out in mumbled syllables.

Blake grabbed her arm and pulled her to the back of the car.

Whitney crouched next to him.

He hugged her against his body. "Are you okay?"

"I'm fine." Her attention jumped to Mike and Sofia crouched by the tree. Thank God everyone was okay and accounted for. None of them could handle another loss.

Suddenly one of the jeeps exploded with a deafening roar. Two rebels catapulted in the air and somersaulted into the ditch. Metal and glass rained down as orange flames licked the night sky.

The glow of the blast outlined Hal as he ran down the road like a movie action hero and shot the last rebel in the back.

* * *

Four hours later, the top of the yellow flight tower at Gerardo Tobar López Airport came into view in the distance. Fluffy white clouds blew across the blue sky along the Pacific coast as sea birds squawked and scouted the shoreline for their next meal.

Blake hung his arm out the car window. Warm air touched his skin and ruffled his hair. He checked the rearview mirror for the hundredth time, happy to see that no one was following them. His muscles finally relaxed and the tension in his shoulders and neck vanished.

They were almost there. Almost home.

He glanced at Whitney next to him. Her skin looked pale in the sunlight and her eyes were dull with exhaustion. She was still very much on edge the way she wrung her hands in her lap. At the very least Whitney would have one hell of a story to tell when she returned to work.

He loosened his grip on the steering wheel. "Not much longer."

"I can't wait to shower and change my clothes." She looked at her jogging suit then at him. Her eyebrows rose. "Tomato red was never my color."

Blake laughed. He was happy her sense of humor had returned.

"How are your ears?"

"Still ringing a bit. I've got one heck of a headache. I don't want to be that close to a stun grenade again."

"Blake, will I be able to go to school in the United States?" Sofia asked.

"Yes, of course. Whichever school you would like." Blake felt sorry for her. She was going to get quite the culture shock after living all her life in Colombia. He had faith she'd adjust just fine. It would take time, though.

Blake wheeled the car into a parking spot at the back of the airport, not wanting to draw attention to their vehicle riddled with bullet holes. He shut off the ignition. Relief flooded through him. They'd made it. Now all they had to do was get through the airport and on that flight home.

Motorcycles zoomed in and out of the lot and various shades of yellow cabs were parked at the curb outside a long butter colored building with reddish-brown trim. An airplane engine roared and whined in the distance. He prayed that was their flight out.

After they all exited the vehicle, Blake spotted a tall woman with stylish short black hair dressed in tight jeans and a loose army green T-shirt holding a cardboard sign with the name 'Jackson Davis' written on it. "There's our contact."

Whitney brushed the hair out of her eyes. "Jackson Davis? I kind of like it. Very cowboyish."

"I knew you would."

Hal patted Mike on his shoulder and grinned. "Our contact's a woman. A damn fine looking one at that."

Whitney laughed and shook her head. She grabbed Sofia's hand.

As they approached, the woman put down the sign then lowered her sunglasses. "I'm Angela Donahue. We need to hurry. The news of Pablo Sanchez's death is just starting to trickle down the ranks. No telling what will happen next." She pulled out a folded piece of paper from her back pocket and handed it to Blake. "Thought you might want this as a memento. It was posted on the wall inside the airport."

He unfolded the paper. It was the wanted poster.

Whitney shot him a bewildered look.

He probably should have told her about the bounty but he didn't want to worry her. She'd been through enough. His attention turned back to Angela. "How are we going to get through airport security? We don't have our passports."

"It's all been looked after. Money talks in this country. Especially US dollars. Just follow me."

Blake couldn't help but wonder how much Chambers had paid to get them out of the country. If only Oscar was here with them.

While Mike and Hal followed Angela to the entrance of the airport, Whitney grabbed Blake's arm and stopped him.

"Are you sure about this? We don't know anything about this woman."

"Chambers set it up. It's on the up and up. Don't worry." He wrapped his arm around her shoulder and kissed her temple. "We're going home."

CHAPTER TWENTY

After landing at McCarran Airport in Las Vegas, Blake went home and showered. Confident that Whitney and Sofia were safe with the help of Mike and Hal, he drove to Ely State Prison to finish what Nathan Shaw had started.

Usually, he detested prisons. Hated the smell. Hated the noise. Today was different. He was alive. Whitney was alive, and he couldn't wait to see the wide-eyed weirdo's face when he walked into the prison visiting area.

A burly guard looked up from behind the glass. "Who you here to see?"

"Nathan Shaw."

The man turned and made a phone call to the cell block. Then Blake heard him say, "Send Inmate Shaw to the visiting room."

"Empty your pockets and put everything in a locker."

As Blake did as he was told, an overhead florescent light bulb buzzed. The sound frayed his nerves. When he was done removing the contents of his pockets another guard escorted him to the windowless visiting area with a low ceiling, old paint and poor ventilation. At the far end, two guards patrolled the area while another guard surveyed the scene from a platform above.

"Sit here. It'll be a few minutes," the guard said.

Blake sat on one of the uncomfortable blue molded plastic chairs and rested his elbows on the scratched table. Twenty minutes passed and he spotted Shaw in the doorway, his feet shackled and his hands cuffed together in front of him. A guard led him to the table.

He took a seat across from Blake and tilted his head. "It's always such a pleasure to see you. Did you find our Miss Steel?"

"Of course I found Whitney. Your plan didn't work. But thanks to you a good friend of mine was killed. His blood is now on your hands. I won't forget that."

"I have no idea what you're talking about. You really have to be so careful anymore, especially in a country plagued by drugs and rebels. Sometimes things get out of hand and horrible things happen. I'm sure that's what happened to your friend."

There was no way the man would ever admit his involvement. That much he knew. Blake shoved his chair away from the table in fear he'd strangle the lying bastard. He stopped himself in mid-thought. "Oh, by the way. Your friend Pablo Sanchez is dead. Think about that while you wither away on death row for the next ten to fifteen years. How old will you be then? Seventy? Seventy-five?"

"Don't be so sure of yourself." Shaw placed his cuffed hands on the table. Perspiration trickled down his temples. "While you and Miss Steel were gallivanting around the world, my new lawyer filed an appeal. Haven't you heard the wonderful news?"

"What news?"

"It seems that Mr. Demotteo, as brilliant and as well paid as he was, had mistakenly hired a retired civil engineer to testify about the gun evidence at my trial. The man wasn't much of an expert if you ask me. Luckily, the Nevada Supreme Court felt the same way." Nathan smirked. "They granted a certiorari to review the issue two days ago."

Blake gritted his teeth. "What the hell does that mean?"

"What it means is—there's an excellent likelihood of a retrial. Without a qualified and competent defense expert in forensic firearms identification my lawyer, Mr. Demotteo, did not provide adequate representation." Nathan edged forward. The shackles around his feet jangled. "Don't ever underestimate me, Barnett. You think you have the upper hand? You don't. You never have and never will."

Retrial? He couldn't believe what he just heard. The bastard had masterminded all of it. Shaw's lawyer knew exactly what he was doing. The guy was a year from retiring anyway. He'd taken the fall to ensure his client would get a retrial and with it—a possible life sentence instead of the death sentence. He wondered how much Shaw had paid Demotteo. Nausea bubbled in his gut. He thought about Whitney. She'd be devastated by the news. Then he thought about his sister, Claire. Nathan Shaw had destroyed so many other lives as well. Mason Bailey, George Raines, Kate Leathham, and Oscar. When would it end? Blake knew as long as Nathan Shaw was alive it wouldn't end.

He'd had enough. If he didn't leave the prison now he'd hop across the table and kill the man. Blake stood. His hands balled into fists and his voice transformed into a low growl. "Don't ever understatement me, Shaw. You might think you're in control. Remember—accidents happen in prison every day."

❋ ❋ ❋

Back at the house, Blake sat beside Whitney on the couch in the great room. The warmth of her body next to his was soothing. It was good to be home. She leaned her head against his shoulder. Her freshly washed hair smelled like watermelon and strawberries. She'd changed into a pair of jeans and a tight white tank top. His pulse ratcheted up two notches. She looked sexy as hell.

Mike and Hal had gone home to shower and to get some sleep. Everyone was exhausted except for Sofia. She was busy in the kitchen, excited to show off her culinary skills. Even though she'd lost her father she was trying to put on a brave face, but Blake knew deep down she was hurting more than he could imagine. He wasn't sure what the young woman was cooking but it smelled delicious.

Blake's stomach growled. "Whatever Sofia is cooking sure smells good."

"It does. She's really a sweet girl. Very smart. Maybe one day she'll own her own restaurant. Oh, I forgot to tell you. When you were in the shower, I called Jerry. He's doing great. The doctor said he will be able to go back to work in a few weeks."

"That's great, honey. I bet you can't wait to get back to work too. Your boss was really worried about you. As much as I was."

Whitney smiled. "I love you. Can I ask you something?"

"Shoot."

"Do you think there might be a chance my father is alive, that he didn't die in Colombia like I was told? It's bothering me what Alejandro said."

"I doubt it. I think he really wanted to get under your skin and nothing more."

"I really don't know. My stomach is telling me something different but it doesn't make sense. If my father was alive—why has he never contacted me?"

"I agree, it doesn't make sense. If it would make you feel better, I can have a couple of my contacts poke around and see if we can find out more."

"Yes, please do. I just have this unsettled feeling I can't shake. I always have. Something just doesn't feel right. I can't explain it."

"Done. I'll look after it tomorrow." He couldn't put it off any longer. Whitney deserved to know. He held her tighter. "We do need to talk about a couple of other things before Angel and my parents get here." He took a drink of his beer then set the bottle on the coffee table.

She lifted her head. Worry lines crinkled her forehead. "Please tell me this is good news not bad."

"Unfortunately, it's not." His mouth turned dry as dirt. He had to tell her everything. She'd learn the truth sooner or later. "Nathan Shaw is probably going to be re-tried."

She abruptly sat up, her eyes huge. "Are you kidding? How?"

Her horrified expression said it all. "I wish I was kidding. Something about his lawyer not providing adequate representation. If he does win the appeal and is retried, there's a good chance he could get a life sentence instead of the death sentence."

"How could this happen?" Her lower lip trembled. "Is he ever going to be out of our lives?"

The image of Oscar dying dashed though his mind.

Nathan Shaw would pay.

Blake didn't know how, but he would. "He will be. The bastard has done enough damage and ruined enough lives."

"I just can't believe this. I'm speechless."

"Honey, there's more."

"Great."

"Before Pablo died he said killing him won't stop anything—that there are thousands on the cartel's payroll and we wouldn't be safe here."

"What are we going to do? We have Angel and Sofia to think about."

He detected the panic in her eyes and heard the fear in her voice, the way her voice quivered. He grabbed her hand and held it tight. "I'll have the security system upgraded and then after the wedding, it might be a good idea for us to take off for awhile—fly under the radar until things settle down."

She looked away for a long moment then down at her engagement ring. "Maybe we should postpone the wedding."

"No way. Not a chance." Blake pulled her to him and wrapped his arms around her. "We're getting married, Whitney. Nothing or no one is going to stop us."

CHAPTER
TWENTY-ONE

Three weeks later...

In the hotel's special reception wedding suite, Whitney adjusted the ivory chiffon strap on her wedding dress and straightened the corsage on the vintage velvet ribbon belt. "Angel, hurry. The photographer is waiting." She turned and checked the back of her dress in the mirror. She couldn't believe it. She had married Blake on the private wraparound terrace overlooking Las Vegas an hour ago, the view magically breathtaking in the early evening light.

"I'll be out soon," Angel yelled from the bathroom.

After learning there was a chance the cartel might still come after them, Whitney had decided to change the venue and downsize the guest list from over two hundred to a much smaller and more intimate affair with less than forty guests and added security. It wasn't the traditional wedding she had already planned before she was kidnapped, but it wasn't about details. It was about family, friends, and the man she loved.

Sofia stood beside her with her dark hair styled in a trendy updo, dressed in a floor length blush pink v-neck chiffon dress looking movie star glamorous with the pearl jewelry Whitney had lent her. Oscar would be proud.

"I really love your watch. It's gorgeous."

"Thank you." Whitney glanced at the white gold and diamond watch. Her heart squeezed. "My father gave it to me when I was a teenager after my mother died." She pushed her hair behind one ear and dangled the teardrop shaped gold earrings. "And these used to belong to my mother."

"When I get married my dad is going..." Her eyes glossed over.

"Sweetie, I'm sorry. I wish he was here too." Whitney put her arm around Sofia's shoulder and gave her a hug. "Your father would be so proud of you. Blake and I are proud of you. You're a beautiful young woman in college. Honey, when you do get married, Blake will walk you down the aisle. I promise."

Her eyes lit up. "Really?"

"Of course. I also know your mom is going to want some pictures of you looking so stunning. We'll send some to her tomorrow."

Angel barreled out of the bathroom and twirled in her gold sequined tulle dress. "I'm ready for pictures." She shoved the baby's-breath crown back on her head then brushed her curly blonde hair off her forehead. Her round blue eyes beamed with mischief.

She ran to Whitney. "You know what?"

"What?"

"I'm happy you're back from working. You worked for a long time. I think I really missed you."

She picked up Angel and kissed her cheek. "I missed you too."

"When the party is done, do I have to go on a mini-vacation again?" She cocked her head and stared at Whitney's face.

Whitney figured the little girl was talking about having to stay at the safe house. She prayed Angel wouldn't ever have to in the future—but there were no guarantees. No guarantees for any of them. With the adoption finally finalized, she didn't want to think about the past. Today was about the future. "Let's not worry about that right now because in six more sleep nights you are coming to live with us."

"Live with you and Blake like forever and ever?"

"Well." Whitney put her down. "I think at least until you get married one day too."

Angel twirled again and pranced up the hallway. "Okay."

After the photographer finished taking their pictures they all returned to the reception.

Whitney sipped a glass of champagne and gazed around the room. Everyone seemed to be having a great time.

As the DJ played song after song, four US Marshals provided security and mingled with some of the guests. Blake was in the corner talking to Trent Chambers, probably filling him in on what went on in Colombia while Cally and McBride were hanging out at the bar with Jerry and Michelle.

Hal was dancing with newfound friend, Angela Donahue, who looked drop dead gorgeous in a short black and white cocktail dress. By the looks of the two grinning at each other, there appeared to be quite a connection. Mike was sitting at a table with his date, a pretty redhead with mile long legs. They were chatting back and forth, laughing and drinking beers.

Blake's mother had a full glass of wine in her hand. She was clearly tipsy as her husband tried to guide her off the dance floor.

Sofia and Angel were smiling and dancing to an upbeat song. The sight warmed Whitney's heart and she thought about how lucky she was. If Blake and the guys hadn't rescued her, she wouldn't be here right now.

Across the room, she spotted him walking toward her with a beer in his hand. The breath caught in her throat. He looked so handsome and sexy in his black tux, white shirt, and pink tie. He had the cutest grin on his face and happiness sparkled in his eyes under the soft lights in the room.

"There's my beautiful wife." He slid his arm around her back then kissed her.

The feel of his mouth on hers sent a burst of fiery heat throughout her body. Her heart flipped.

"Have I told you how much I love you today?"

"You have. But you can always tell me again."

"Whitney Steel. I love you with all my heart, body, and soul."

AUTHOR'S NOTE

I hope you enjoyed reading *Retribution* as much as I enjoyed writing the story. Please don't forget to leave a review.

I have some fantastic news! Blake and Whitney's story is not over yet!

Buy *Resurrect* (A Whitney Steel Novel – Book Three) today!

Special thanks to Authors Stacy Green and Kat Flannery for taking time out of their busy schedules to review *Retribution*. I hope you check out these talented authors. You won't be disappointed.

To my fans, readers and reviewers—thank you for your continuing support!

You rock!

www.ingramcontent.com/pod-product-compliance
Lightning Source LLC
Chambersburg PA
CBHW071140170626
46809CB00002B/701